Share the Fire

The Toronto Blessing and Grace-Based Evangelism

Guy Chevreau

Preface by John Arnott, Senior Pastor
of the Toronto Airport Christian Fellowship

Revival Press

An Imprint of
Destiny Image® Publishers, Inc.
P.O. Box 310
Shippensburg, PA 17257-0310

ISBN 1-56043-688-3
(Previously published by author under ISBN 0-9681642-0-X)

For Worldwide Distribution
Printed in the U.S.A.

This book and all other Destiny Image, Revival Press,
and Treasure House books are available
at Christian bookstores and distributors worldwide.

For a U.S. bookstore nearest you, call **1-800-722-6774**.
For more information on foreign distributors,
call **717-532-3040**.
Or reach us on the Internet: **http://www.reapernet.com**

Acknowledgments

It has been two years and one month since I sent *Catch the Fire* off to HarperCollins. In Sydney, Australia, I received a prophetic word of encouragement that the Lord purposed three books in two years. With the completion of *Share the Fire*, that word has come to pass. My heavenly Father has been so very faithful and so incredibly gracious to me.

What a tremendous privilege to be part of this move of God's Spirit! It has literally swept the earth these last 34 months, and as the Lord has called me to travel to 15 different countries, and over 50 different cities, I am so grateful to my hosts. They have been some of the most godly, humble, obedient, generous, and Christ-like men and women I have ever had the pleasure of meeting. So many have become such very good friends. Thank you for your love and acceptance.

To those who are freely giving away what they have freely received, those who are sharing good news with the poor, serving the outcasts, befriending the stranger, and caring for the fatherless, I bless you in the name of Jesus. It has been an honor to walk with you, even for the briefest of moments. Thank you to all those who released their testimonies for publication.

The Toronto Airport Christian Fellowship is our home church. Our debt of gratitude to the people there is immense.

To the staff, both pastoral and support, as well as to the church body, the words *thank you* are impoverished.

On the home front, it feels as though we've shifted from one unexpectedly extended sprint and begun to pace things for a longer run. So much has changed for us as a family. Janis, Graham, and Caitlin, I cannot say it often enough: you are cherished and precious gifts. I love you so much.

Final thanks go to Dr. Barry Morrison—your critical comments on the drafts helped sharpen the focus. To Alan Wiseman—again, bless you for your faithful intercession and prophetic encouragement.

Guy Chevreau
Oakville, Ontario
October 1996

Contents

"I count myself one of the number of those who
write as they learn
and learn as they write."

Augustine[1]

---

1.   Augustine, *Letters*, trans. by J.G. Pilkerton. Nicene and Post-Nicene
Fathers, First Series, vol. 1 (Peabody, Massachusetts: Hendrickson
Publishers, 1994), 490.

Preface

Three years after the initial outbreak of revival in our Toronto church, many of us have had opportunity to have significant involvement in nurturing, spreading, and sharing the fire of God, not only in our own backyard, but in numerous nations and denominations around the world. We have seen a tiny flame grow into a vast and glorious "forest fire" for the Kingdom of God. As God has poured out His Spirit, so many people have received what we call "the Father's Blessing."

Dr. Guy Chevreau is one who has traveled the globe during this time, sharing his delightful and powerful insights with the Body of Christ, with those who are hungry and eager not only to learn more, but also to surrender their lives in this great move of the Holy Spirit. His first book, *Catch the Fire* has served so well to introduce many leaders and laymen alike to the intensity of the Holy Spirit's ministry and to the physical manifestations that so often accompany His presence. Guy has also served us in demonstrating that the manifestations we see today are so very similar to those that characterized historical revivals of previous centuries. With his grounding in the Scriptures, he has always pointed beyond the manifestations and helped us to focus on the abundance of good fruit.

In his second book, *Pray With Fire*, Guy helped resource us further, as we attend to what the Spirit continuously calls forth from us. It was sobering to learn that it has always been revivals' best friends that have killed things! To surrender our agendas and discern what is on God's has been one of our foremost concerns these last three years.

Guy's study of revelatory ministry has also served us well, for the release of prophetic giftings is one of the key dynamics to all that the Lord purposes in this outpouring.

As we have talked, Guy and I agree that the greatest and most needed revelation that must come to the Church is that of the Father's great love for us, individually as well as corporately. Eternal life and indeed everything we receive from the Father is His gift of grace. It is expressed through Christ's saving and healing love, which cannot be earned, deserved, or bought. It is nothing of works, lest any should boast (see Eph. 2:8-9). Rather, it is a love that sets the captives free. It is the very nature and heart of the Father to freely give of Himself and His blessings to those of us who are least deserving.

I remember the time that I did not realize the full significance of the word *grace*. To me it sounded like a term other religions would use or something that theologians would talk about. It was a "Christianese" word that was often heard yet seldom understood. It was revelation to me when I learned that the word simply means "gift," from *charis* in ancient Greek.

This free gift of grace is the foundation of Dr. Chevreau's new book *Share the Fire*. Again Guy has served us as he addresses one of the questions we are most frequently asked: "Where is all of this going?" We believe that our Father purposes the greatest ingathering of souls that the world has ever seen. The Lord of the Harvest has waited patiently for His harvest to come in, and there will be a grace-based evangelism that goes into the highways and byways and compels the lost to come in. It truly is "Amazing Grace."

This book will help equip you and encourage you to believe that our God, who is mighty to save, wants now to reap the earth (see Rev. 14:16). With great anticipation for an imminent and unprecedented harvest, I heartily recommend this work to you.

John Arnott, Senior Pastor
Toronto Airport Christian Fellowship

About the Author

Dr. Guy Chevreau served the Baptist Church from 1979 to 1994. With a B.A. in philosophy, and a Masters of Divinity from Acadia Divinity College, he received his Th.D. from Wycliffe College, Toronto School of Theology, having studied in the area of historical theology. In September of 1994, he became part of the renewal team based at the Toronto Airport Christian Fellowship, serving international conferences.

Guy is the author of *Catch the Fire*, which sets what has come to be known as the "Toronto Blessing" in some biblical and historical contexts, and complements these studies with present-day testimonies of the impartation of God's grace and love that hundreds of thousands have received through this remarkable outpouring of the Spirit. Since its release in October 1994, *Catch the Fire* has been translated into nine foreign languages.

Pray With Fire serves as a sequel; its subtitle is "Interceding in the Spirit." Although there are several books that encourage us to pray *for* revival, no other addresses what it means to pray *in the midst* of an outpouring of God's Spirit. And rather than spelling out another methodology for prayer, this book is a call to an ever-deepening relationship with the Lord who wants to speak to us more than we want to speak with Him. In his review, Dr. John White said, "This book spells the difference between praying with fire and playing with it."

Guy is married to Janis; they have two children, Graham and Caitlin. When it's windy enough, Guy is likely to be found out on Lake Ontario, windsurfing.

Chapter 1

Such Groaning and Shouting;
It Sets Me to Doubting

A Prologue

So no place is left for any human pride in the presence of God. By God's act you are in Christ Jesus; God has made Him our wisdom...our holiness, our liberation. Therefore, in the words of scripture, "If anyone must boast, let him boast of the Lord" (1 Corinthians 1:29-31).

* * *

On July 10, 1996, a 25-year-old named Bobby[1] walked into the foyer of the Toronto Airport Christian Fellowship. Bobby had lived on the streets since he was 12, and he had been using and dealing drugs for the last 14 years. He met his Hell's Angel father for the first time when he was 18. His life was, as he described it, "getting high, robbing people, and hurting people." For the past five years, Bobby had been in jail for Christmas. He is functionally illiterate.

This particular afternoon, he was high on crack cocaine and marijuana, and had a loaded gun in his pocket. Needing

---

1. Because of his recent conversion, pastoral staff felt it wisest to use a pseudonym.

money for drugs, he had come to rob the place. Bobby had misunderstood the name of the church, and because of some misinformation, he thought that it was an Italian card and casino club. He figured he'd soon have in his pocket the poker money he expected to steal.

Sandy, the foyer receptionist, was the first one to speak to him. As she looked at him walking in, she had a feeling that he was so very lost, and that he desperately needed to know the Father's love. Bobby said that just standing in the foyer, he was overwhelmed with what he now knows to be the presence of God; what he knew initially was that his drug buzz evaporated. As Sandy and Bobby talked, she invited him to the evening meeting. He said, "You wouldn't want my kind here." She asked why. He answered, "I'm a criminal." Sandy assured him that he was more than welcome. He responded that there wasn't any hope for him, and that his family had given up on him. Again, Sandy invited him to the meeting, feeling an urgency to say something more. She looked into his eyes and said, "God really loves you." Bobby was stunned, and became choked up with tears; he panicked and headed back out the door.

Outside, he sat down on the curb, his head in his hands. Some time later, a man came and sat beside him. They talked. Bobby had tears in his eyes. The man suggested that he come to the meeting later that night. He got some sleep behind one of the local warehouses, and after he had smoked a couple of joints to bolster his courage, he made his way into the meeting. That night, when the salvation call was issued, he gave his life to Jesus. Hours later, as he had done so many other nights, he slept on a picnic bench.

Over the course of the next month, Bobby was befriended by and incorporated into the young adults group at the church and began to be discipled. Several of them stood with him through his bail hearing; others helped him find work; and still others are helping him manage his money. He stayed with one of the pastors for three weeks until other accommodations could be arranged, and new friends have come alongside as he re-orients his drug-free lifestyle.

On August 17, Bobby publicly proclaimed his faith in Jesus Christ as his Savior and Lord in the waters of baptism. When asked about some of the changes Bobby has noticed since his conversion, he quickly answered, "I'm a 100 percent different. Instead of take, I give. I believe in the Lord; He's my God, He's number one in my life, and He's the One looking after me. The drugs are gone, the alcohol is gone, the violence is gone.... All that stuff is gone. I'm a new person. It's great."

As of October 1996, Bobby was off to Teen Challenge, a Christian drug rehabilitation program, for a year of discipleship. Upon graduation, he hopes to go back to the streets and share the love of God with the homeless.

* * *

The vast majority of those visiting the Toronto Airport Christian Fellowship have come with markedly different motives than Bobby's. But many have been met no less dramatically. *The Toronto Star*'s Faith and Ethics newspaper reporter began her story on the second "Catch the Fire" conference, held in October 1995:

> "The mighty winds of hurricane Opal that swept through Toronto last week were mere tropical gusts compared with the power of God thousands believe struck them senseless at a conference of the controversial Airport Vineyard Church."

She continued:

> "At least with Opal, they could stay on their feet. Not so with many of the 5,300 souls meeting at the Regal Constellation Hotel. The ballroom carpets were littered with fallen bodies, bodies of seemingly straight-laced men and

women, who felt themselves moved by the phenomenon they say is the Holy Spirit. So moved, they howled with joy or the release of some long buried pain. They collapsed, some rigid as corpses, some convulsed in hysterical laughter. From room to room come barnyard cries, calls heard only in the wild, grunts so deep women recalled the sounds of childbirth, while some men and women adopted the very position of childbirth."[2]

Four months later, the Toronto Airport Christian Fellowship was again in the headlines: *The post-Toronto phenomenon— when have we laughed enough and can go back to work?*

"Most of the churches worldwide which have been affected by the Toronto-phenomenon are going through a phase of re-orientation. The attitude of most pastors we meet is 'We tried it, it didn't hurt, but it didn't help much either.' Beside the many positive reports in the areas of counseling, self-discovery and honesty, and the extremely few reports in the areas of evangelization and mission, there is now a fear growing in many churches that 'the Toronto phenomenon' could become institutionalized.

"Many blessings have died as people tried to control it, organize it or to manipulate it to fit their personal beliefs. The Bible has no problems with people falling over, but it values more what they do when they stand up again. Whether we rest in the spirit [sic] or our flesh, there are still three billion completely unreached people in the world, of which the majority is under 15, people under the poverty line and in slums waiting to hear the gospel.

"Let's go together—as blessed as possible—to bring them this blessing."[3]

---

2. Leslie Scrivener, *The Toronto Star*, October 8, 1995: A2.

3. *Island Herald*, February 1996.

The "Toronto Blessing" has received a great deal of media attention from both secular and religious sources. The two clips above are suggestive of the diverse ways in which many are reacting. Those outside the Church are characteristically intrigued with such dynamic happenings taking place in the lives of people whom the press has tended to marginalize, if not ignore. Many inside the Church have misunderstood and even misrepresented this outpouring of God's Spirit, as in the *Island Herald* article, referring to the Blessing as "it."

The powerful, loving presence of God, however, is not an "it." John Arnott, the senior pastor of the Toronto Airport Christian Fellowship, continually pushes this to the forefront, even titling his book *The Father's Blessing*. The "heart" of what hundreds of thousands have discovered is that the Master and Creator of the universe has chosen to reveal Himself as tender, gracious, and merciful; He has come, at His own initiative, seeking the likes of us; He continuously lays blessing over the cursedness of our lives; and He invites us into an ever-deepening relationship with Himself. This revelation is the very gospel of Jesus Christ. In any given moment, the personal and corporate life transformations that result are at the core of Christian faith, regardless of the physical posture one assumes. The falling and the other physical manifestations characterizing this move of the Spirit have been provocative, at the very least.

Introduction to the Toronto Blessing

Although major conferences are hosted about every other month, regular meetings are held six nights a week at the Toronto Airport Christian Fellowship (TACF). (Prior to January 20, 1996, the name of the church was the Toronto Airport Vineyard.) These meetings were initiated when a Vineyard pastor, Randy Clark of St. Louis, was invited to preach over a long weekend in January of 1994.

Currently, nightly congregations at the TACF average between 700 to 1,200 per night, and are drawn from literally every corner of the globe and virtually every denomination of the Body of Christ. Over 50,000 pastors have come from all over continental North America, Britain, Germany, Iceland, Scandinavia, the Netherlands, Switzerland, Austria, France, Spain, Italy, South Africa, Nigeria, Kenya, East Africa, Swaziland, Korea, Indonesia, Mongolia, Japan, New Zealand, Australia, Chile, Peru, Argentina, Guatemala, Nicaragua…. As those on pilgrimage, they have come to receive what the British secular press nicknamed the "Toronto Blessing."

Those who have come spiritually hungry have experienced a depth of spiritual refreshment, awakening, and release that they are quick to testify that they have experienced a much needed measure of God's grace, and have seen the power of His love, demonstrated and appropriated in personal ways. Thousands of defeated, discouraged, and exhausted Christians have testified that through the Blessing, they've never known so much of God's love for them, nor known so much love for Him. Many have experienced a renewing of commitment and call, an enlarging and clarification of spiritual vision, and a rekindled passion for Jesus and the work of the Kingdom. Thousands of desperate and burned-out pastors and their spouses have been refreshed, recommissioned, and released in new freedom, authority, and power to declare the good news of Jesus Christ.

But it has not been just believers who have formed the nightly congregations. Although they have found this problematic to track, the New Life ministry teams have made contact with at least 8,000 prodigals who have come forward for prayer as they recommit their lives; over 6,000 have made first-time professions of faith. Bobby was one of these.

These are the more consequential dynamics at work in the "Toronto Blessing." What has generated so much of the attention are the physical manifestations that have often accompanied this gracious outpouring of God's Spirit—hysterical laughter, shouting, shaking, and the like. These phenomena have caused some to take such exception to the "Toronto Blessing" that they call it the "Toronto Blasphemy." Such critics are adamant that God does not "do" these sorts of things to His people. However, a close reading of primary records of past, *bona fide* revivals indicates many striking similarities to much of the phenomena that have come to characterize what the guarded have alternatively called the "Toronto Mixed-Blessing."

Wisdom Does Not Judge What It Does Not Understand

As I have continued to research past moves of God, my pre-renewal characterization of historic revivals has been challenged. The typical picture of the Welsh revival, for example, is that of the coal miners coming straight from the pit to the chapel, their blackened faces soon washed with free-flowing tears of repentance. However, a closer and more comprehensive study of the historical record seems to indicate strong precedent for much of what is being experienced by so many as they find themselves "Toronto Blessed." Grawys Jones, a local pastor of Aberdare, Wales, spoke of his experience in the early days of the 1904-1905 revival:

> "Some most strange joy took possession of the whole congregation. The only way I can describe it is this—as if a great shower were coming down the valley here—I have seen it often—and you can hear the noise of it in the wind, and then by and by a few big drops come, the forerunner of the great shower. Exactly like that it came. I knew that something great was approaching."[4]

---

4. Brynmor Pierce Jones, *Voices From the Welsh Revival 1904-1905* (Bridgend: Evangelical Press of Wales, 1995), 174.

Jones described how when the man who was leading in prayer would close, another would start singing, and as the congregation lifted their praise for a quarter of an hour,

> "some were shouting for joy, and others praying. We three ministers in the pulpit were crying for joy, the tears running down our faces. We were lost to everything, and forgot all about this world, I think. The joy of it, the immense, untold joy of it was something that I never, never dreamed possible...."[5]

That particular meeting went late into the night.

> "About 4 o'clock (in the morning) I went home, and I could hear companies in the early morning singing away with all their might. I went to bed but could hardly sleep, and when I did I was laughing for joy in my sleep, and I got up in the morning full of joy."[6]

Such an account is not an isolated mutation of true revival. Written 56 years earlier (1848), the following is a dialogue song between a "Shouting" Methodist and a "Formalist," most likely either a Presbyterian or a Congregationalist. It is a graphic description of the meetings conducted, and reflects a most remarkable similarity to the experience of "Toronto's" friends and sceptics, both the questions raised and the answers given.

The Methodist begins with warm greeting:

> *"Good morning, brother pilgrim! What, trav'ling to Zion?*
> *What doubts and what dangers have you met today?*
> *Have you gain'd a blessing, then pray without ceasing,*
> *Press forward, my brother, and make no delay;*
> *Have you a desire that burns like a fire,*
> *And long for the hour when Christ shall appear?"*

---

5. *Ibid.*
6. *Ibid.*

The Formalist responds by describing his experience at the Methodist's meetings:

"I came out this morning, and now I'm returning,
Perhaps little better than when I first came,
Such groaning and shouting, it sets me to doubting,
I fear such religion is only a dream.
The preachers are stamping, the people are jumping,
And screaming so loud that I nothing could hear,
Either the praying or preaching—such horrible shrieking!
I was truly offended at all that was there."

The Methodist asks after the Formalist's involvement:

"Perhaps, my dear brother, while they prayed together
You sat and considered, but prayed not at all:
Would you find a blessing, then pray without ceasing,
Obey the advice that was given by Paul.
For if you should reason at any such season,
No wonder if Satan should tell in your ear,
That preachers and people are only a rabble,
And this is no place for reflection and prayer."

The Formalist recoils:

"No place for reflection—I'm filled with distraction,
I wonder that people could bear for to stay,
The men they were bawling, the women were squalling,
I know not for my part how any could pray.
Such horrid confusion—if this be religion
I'm sure that it's nothing that never was seen,
For the sacred pages that speak of all ages,
Do nowhere declare that such ever has been."

The Methodist takes over with his apologetic:

"Don't be so soon shaken
if I'm not mistaken
Such things were perform'd by believers of old;
When the ark was coming, King David came running,

And dancing before it, in Scripture we're told.
When the Jewish nation had laid the foundation,
To rebuild the temple at Ezra's command,
Some wept and some praised, such noise there was raised,
'Twas heard afar off and perhaps through the land...."

The Formalist counters:

"Then Scripture's contrasted, for Paul has protested
That order should reign in the house of the Lord,
Amid such a clatter who knows what's the matter?
Or who can attend unto what is declared?
To see them behaving like drunkards, all raving,
And lying and rolling prostrate on the ground,
I really feel awful, and sometimes felt fearful
That I'd be the next that would come tumbling down."

The Methodist gives the following counsel:

"You say you felt awful—you ought to be careful
Lest you grieve the Spirit, and so He depart,
By your own confession, you've felt some impression,
The sweet melting showers have softened your heart.
You fear persecution, and that's a delusion
Brought in by the devil to stop up your way.
Be careful, my brother, for blest are no other
Than persons that 'are not offended in Me.' "

"As Peter was preaching, and bold in his teaching,
The Spirit descended and some were offended,
And said of these men, 'They're filled with new wine.'
I never yet doubted that some of them shouted,
While others lay prostrate, by power struck down;
Some weeping, some praising, while others were saying:
'They're drunkards or fools, or in falsehood abound....' "

He offers to pray for the Formalist, that his "precious
soul would be filled with the fire of God."

How does it end? The Formalist is won over, confident that at very least, God's "mercy is sure unto all that believe." His testimony?

"My heart is now glowing! I feel His love flowing! Peace, pardon, and comfort I now do receive!"[7]

Share the Fire

God has continuously renewed and revived His people, both throughout the pages of the Scriptures, and in the on-going history of His Church. This restoring work has always had a twofold consequence of quality and quantity. Through the "Toronto Blessing," there are thousands of believers worldwide who testify to a deeper, fuller revelation of the Father's loving heart such that a new measure of faith and faithfulness has been awakened within the Church. Perhaps as never before, many recognize the truth declared by the Welsh revivalist, Evan Roberts when he said, "God cannot do a great work *through* you without doing a great work *in* you first."[8] Having been the subjects of the Lord's gracious work, there has been a broader, outgoing revelation of God's love, demonstrated by those who have been revived. Put simply, we more than recognize that God pours out His Spirit not just that we "be blessed," but that we "be a blessing." Writing roughly 850 years ago, the great revival preacher Bernard of Clairvaux put things this way:

> "[The Spirit's] operation in us is twofold. For He not only fortifies us interiorly with virtues, unto our own salvation, but He also adorns us exteriorly with His gifts, unto the salvation of others. The former are bestowed upon us for our own sakes, the latter with a view to our neighbour's

---

7. Winthrop Hudson, *Encounter*, vol. 29 (Winter 1968), 74.
8. Brynmor Pierce Jones, *An Instrument of Revival: The Complete Life of Evan Roberts, 1878-1951* (South Plainfield, New Jersey: Bridge Publishing, 1995), 65.

advantage. For instance, we obtain faith, hope, and charity
for ourselves…and the word of wisdom and knowledge,
the grace of healing, the gift of prophecy, and the
like…which are communicated to be employed in promot-
ing the spiritual interests of others."[9]

* * *

The subtitle of this book is *The Toronto Blessing and
Grace-Based Evangelism.* As thousands of refreshed and renewed pastors, leaders, and churches around the world attend to what the Spirit of the Lord is imparting and calling
forth, there is the recognition that unless "streams of living
water"[10] flow out from within, they will soon stagnate, or
even recede. This recognition, however, could call forth a
striving on our part that would compromise the Lord's purposes in this fresh outpouring of His Spirit. If we were to
work the metaphor Jesus used in John chapter 7, it is not we
who make the stream flow out. We are the recipients of the
living water that flows through us with such a super abundance that there is a wonderful overflow.

The following chapter is a consideration of some of the
dynamics at work in the development of historic revivals.
When studied, a general pattern and process can be discerned: believers and churches were first awakened; in turn,
unbelievers came to faith in Jesus Christ, were incorporated
into His Body, and used to draw others to newness of life.
As with *Catch the Fire* and *Pray With Fire,* the subsequent
chapters bring biblical study, historic precedent, and present testimony to bear, with the view to welding Kingdom
theology, mission, and an outpouring of God's Spirit together.

---

9. *St. Bernard's Sermons on the Canticle of Canticles,* vol. I, "On the Two
    Operations of the Holy Ghost" (Dublin: Browne and Nolan, 1920),
    174-175.
10. John 7:38.

As essentials are clarified and restated, it is hoped that the following resources and reflections will serve to help us steward this precious anointing. With the grace of God ever before us, we recognize, again, that the way on is the same as the way in. Living out this gospel revelation, we are released and empowered to share with others the fire with which we have been baptized. As such, we will be "...like a burning brazier in the woodland [and] like a burning torch among the sheaves."[11]

11. Zechariah 12:6.

Chapter 2

Ripples on the Pond:

The Dynamics of Revival

...'O man, can these bones live?'...'Only You, Lord God,
know that.' ...'Prophecy to the wind, prophecy, O man,
and say to it: These are the words of the Lord God: Let
winds come from every quarter and breathe into these slain,
that they may come to life' (Ezekiel 37:3,9).

* * *

In the pastors and leaders sessions we host at the
Toronto Airport Christian Fellowship, the question is repeatedly raised: "When does all of this move from renewal
to revival?" Here, a word of explanation is required. The
term *renewal* was suggested in the early weeks of the meetings at the Toronto Airport Vineyard, for it was felt that it
would be presumptuous to name things *revival* from the
start. The dynamic consequences of the protracted meetings were for history to evaluate and name. There were others who insisted that the term *revival* cannot be used until
mass conversions are witnessed.

Definitions are critical things. Once named, they become determinative, for they set boundaries and distin-
guish one thing from another. Classically, a "revival of
religion" has been defined as:

"the awakening into more active and living energy those religious feelings, habits, and principles, which previously existed, but which had sunk into comparative dormancy. But that is not all its meaning. It is employed also to indicate the conversion of sinners, who were previously in a state of irreligion altogether.... Revival is to be understood as an unusual manifestation of the power of the grace of God in convincing and converting careless sinners, and in quickening and increasing the faith and piety of believers.... It is the life-giving, light-imparting, quickening, regenerating, and sanctifying energy of the Holy Spirit...."[1]

More recently, Donald McGavran's interpretation of revival may surprise some readers. (McGavran is the author of the "classic" text, *Understanding Church Growth,* and is considered by many as the father of the church growth movement.) He begins by quoting Edwin Orr on "awakening":

"An Evangelical Awakening is a movement of the Holy Spirit *in the Church of Christ* bringing about a revival of New Testament Christianity. Such an awakening may change in a significant way an individual only; or it may affect a larger group of people; or it may move a congregation, or the churches of a city or district, or the whole body of believers throughout the world. Such an awakening may run its course briefly, or it may last a whole lifetime."

McGavran goes on to define revival as:

"God's gift. Human beings can neither command it nor make God grant it. God sovereignly gives revival when and where He wills. It 'breaks out,' 'strikes,' 'quickens a church,' 'comes with the suddenness of a summer storm,' 'makes its appearance,' 'inaugurates a work of grace,' and

1. *The Revival of Religion: Addresses by Scottish Evangelical Leaders.* Edinburgh: The Banner of Truth Trust, 1840/1984: x.

'blesses His people'…. By the very structure of the word, revival means revivification of an existing church or existing Christians. There must be first tired believers before they can be revived. All accounts tell of cold, indifferent, or sinful congregations that, by revival, are kindled to new consecration…. If the significant meaning of the word— vitalizing an existing church—is to be preserved, it must not be used for the original turnings of non-Christians to Christ."[2]

Historically, a "quickening and increase" of faith is often seen first in the church's leadership. Revival scholar Iain Murray documents the "striking change" people saw in their preachers as they were "awakened." For example, the ministry of the Presbyterian pastor, William Graham, of Lexington, Virginia, was described as both "able and orthodox." While at the revival meetings that were sweeping the Blue Ridge Mountains in August 1789, Graham "was as a man suddenly transformed." In his subsequent preaching, there was a recognized increase in authority, warmth, and joy. So too, with John Blair Smith, who was described as "a popular preacher…but for years, his preaching seemed to take no effect, there was no awakening of sinners, no arousing of cold professors (believers), nor reclaiming of backsliders. But at the commencement of the great revival of 1786/7, he underwent a remarkable change in his own feelings and in the fervency of his preaching so that he became one of the most powerful preachers I ever heard."[3] The same is said of the change that came over the Rev. Dr. John McDonald, a Scottish revival preacher:

---

2. Donald McGavran, *Understanding Church Growth*, 3rd ed. (Grand Rapids, Michigan: William B. Eerdmans Pub. Co., 1990), 134-135, 139. Italics added.

3. Iain H. Murray, *Revival and Revivalism: The Making and Marring of American Evangelism 1750-1858* (Edinburgh: The Banner of Truth Trust, 1994), 107.

"There have been instances of persons becoming 'other men' who were never new creatures in Christ; but there have been also instances of renewed men becoming other men under a fresh baptism of the Spirit. This was the change which Mr. McDonald underwent in Edinburgh. It was soon apparent in his preaching. Always clear and sound in his statements of objective truth, his preaching had now become instinct with life. It was now searching and fervent, as well as sound and lucid.... His statements of gospel truth were now the warm utterances of one who deeply felt its power. The Lord's people could now testify that he spoke from his own heart to theirs."

Murray concludes the chapter with this assessment:

"The Great Revival taught the Presbyterian churches that orthodoxy and correct preaching, indispensable though they are, are not enough. Authority, tenderness, compassion, pity—these must be given in larger measure from heaven, and when they are it can truly be said that theology has taken fire.... The facts are indisputable. A considerable body of men, for a long period before the Second Great Awakening, preached the same message as they did during the revival but with vastly different consequences— the same men, the same actions, performed with the same abilities, yet the results were so amazingly different!"[4]

The First Link in the Chain of Grace

To use McGavran's terms, there has come through the "Toronto Blessing" a most remarkable "revivification of existing Christians and churches." Although there is no possible way of knowing how many individuals have formed the evening congregations, over one million people have cumulatively attended the Toronto Airport Christian Fellowship, as

---

4. *Ibid.*, 109, 127.

of May 1996. This milestone marked the fact that thousands and thousands of pastors, leaders, and believers from around the world have been refreshed, renewed, and awakened. Historically, this is the precursor, the forerunner, to what most understand as "classic" revival.

For instance, when the Great Awakening first began in Northampton, conversions were recorded, but the most predominant awakening was that of the Church. In his *A Faithful Narrative of the Surprising Work of God in the Conversion of Many Hundred Souls in Northampton and the Neighbouring Towns,* Jonathan Edwards noted that in late December 1734, "the Spirit of God began to extraordinarily set in," and five or six persons were "savingly converted, some of them wrought upon in a very remarkable manner." Referring to the restorative prophecy in Ezekiel 37:1-14, he goes on to say that such glorious work caused a stir within the church: "the noise amongst the dry bones waxed louder and louder"; by the summer of 1735, this work of God had made "a glorious alteration in the town, such that it seemed to be full of the presence of God." He states: "Those among us who had been formerly converted, were greatly enlivened, and renewed with fresh and extraordinary [experiences] of the Spirit of God; though some much more than others, according to the measure of the gift of Christ. Many who had laboured under difficulties about their own [spiritual] state, now had their doubts removed by more satisfying experience, and more clear discoveries of God's love."[5]

He says of the preaching,

"the arguments are the same that they have heard hundreds of times; but the force of the arguments, and their

5. *The Collected Works of Jonathan Edwards* (Edinburgh: The Banner of Truth Trust, 1992), I.348ab.

conviction by them, is altogether new; they come with a new and before unexperienced power. Before, they heard it was so, and they allowed it to be so; but now they see it to be so indeed.... Persons after their conversions often speak of religious things as seeming new to them; that preaching is a new thing; that it seems to them they never heard preaching before; that the Bible is a new book; they find there new chapters, new psalms, new histories, because they see them in a new light."[6]

Along with this internal awakening within the church, Edwards conservatively estimated that in the first six months of the revival, 300 souls were "savingly brought home to Christ."

Joseph Tracy carefully studied the Great Awakening 100 years after its occurrence. He describes the congregations that gathered to hear Edwards preach his extended sermon series on justification by faith:

"The preacher had before him a considerable number of men, who were in no respect regarded or treated as regenerate persons; who were regarded, both by the church and by themselves, as unrenewed, impenitent men, destitute of faith, and of every Christian grace, and in the broad road to perdition. It was not merely feared or believed that the congregation contained many such persons. The church records contained the names of those who were supposed to be in the road to heaven; and others were, by common consent, to be regarded and addressed as persons in the road to hell."[7]

The theological backdrop to this situation was that a pragmatic Arminianism had been taught for years—such

---

6. *Ibid.*, I.356ab.
7. Joseph Tracy, *The Great Awakening: A History of the Revival...* (Edinburgh: The Banner of Truth Trust, 1842/1989), 4, 391-392.

that well-intentioned, but unconverted, men and women believed that they could, without supernatural grace, live an
ethical and social life that would be pleasing to God, and
that those who were doing so, were doing very well. Edwards made it clear that the gravity of sin, and the peril of
an uncertain profession of faith in Christ's saving grace
made such "works righteousness" a spiritual folly. Of the results of Edwards' passionate preaching, Tracy brings forward the following critical assessments:

> "Great numbers of church members were converted. We
> must remember that the practice of admitting to the com-
> munion all persons neither heretical nor scandalous, was
> general in the Presbyterian church, and prevailed exten-
> sively among the Congregational churches. In conse-
> quence, a large proportion of the communicants in both
> were unconverted persons. Multitudes of these were con-
> verted.... In some cases, the revival seems to have been al-
> most wholly within the church, and have resulted in the
> conversion of nearly all the members.... These converted
> church members, from want of their piety, were at best
> dead weights to the churches. They now became active
> and valuable members.

> "There was a twofold gain. In every such instance, the
> church felt its encumbering burden diminished, and its
> strength increased."[8]

History Repeats Itself

Similar dynamics are traced in a subsequent move of the
Spirit. Prior to the Second Great Awakening, church life
in general was described as "cold and dead." In 1760,
churches of Baptist persuasion were "few in number and of
negligible influence." One Virginian Christian declared,

---

8. *Ibid.*

"too many Presbyterians were sound in doctrine but deficient in experience."[9] In the early years of the 1800's, God graciously poured out His Spirit, especially through camp meetings like the ones held in Cane Ridge, Kentucky. The situation *slowly, but dynamically*, began to change. Of the estimated 10,000 people in the meetings in August of 1801, 144 conversions were recorded—a fairly small yield.

However, a local Baptist church nearby had added only six to the church in the five years that preceded the outpouring, but two years after the summer meetings, that one fellowship added 320 new members. A sister church had been static for 19 years; in the two years following the camp meetings, they baptized 318 new believers. The nearby Elkhorn Association of Baptist Churches was made up of 27 churches, and in 1800, had 1,642 members. Two years after the outpouring, 21 new churches had begun, membership having more than tripled.

Thirty, Sixty, a Hundred Fold

These statistics are only to demonstrate the exponential, slowly starting, but dynamically gaining growth patterns in revival. This is exactly the description of the growth pattern of the Kingdom, as Jesus said it would be in teachings such as the parables of the sower, the mustard seed, and the leaven.[10] There is, as it were, botanical progression here. God releases a fresh outpouring of gifts, resources, and a dynamic empowerment for ministry, but these take some time to "take root" before they "bear fruit." In terms of evangelism, this is especially the case. One unbeliever comes to Christ and is nurtured in his or her faith. Over the next weeks and months, this zealous evangelist witnesses to

---

9.   Iain Murray, *Op. cit.*, 65, 93.
10. Matthew 13:8,32-33.

unchurched family and friends. As they see the qualitative life transformation evidenced as the new believer lives his or her life in Christ, there is a credible and dynamic witness which leads to further conversions, sometimes of whole families and friendship networks.

In 1770 there were fewer than 1,000 American Methodists. By 1820, 50 years later, there were over 250,000. There was both remarkable spiritual growth and a tremendous influx of immigrants from the "old" world. To work the statistics in a different way, in 1775 one out of every 800 Americans was a Methodist; by 1812 it was one out of every 36.[11] That, despite—or in part because of—congregational behavior that Anglican missionary Charles Woodmason described thus: "Gang[s] of frantic Lunatics broke out of Bedlam.... One on his knees in a Posture of Prayer—Others singing—some howling—These Ranting—Those Crying—Others dancing, Skipping, Laughing and rejoicing."[12] Wigger comments, "While early Methodism cannot be reduced to enthusiasm, neither can it be understood without it."[13]

The Tension

A blessed season of revival may require greater discernment than any other period of church life. The "Toronto Blessing" is not about the manifestations—but rather, it is about the Father blessing His children. Having firmly established that central declaration, we have to be quick to say that the "Toronto Blessing" cannot be understood without the manifestations. Eifion Evans traces this same tension at work in the Welsh revival of 1904-1905:

---

11. John H. Wigger, "Taking Heaven by Storm," *Journal of the Early Republic*, 14 (Summer 1994), 167.
12. *Ibid.*, 177.
13. *Ibid.*, 191.

"Oh, what a scene it was! The whole place was in apparent confusion, some praying aloud, others confessing their sins, many of the heathen in agony appealing to God for pardon, some even fainted, so great was the power. It was a pleasure to hear some of the older Christians praising God and shouting, 'The Church now lives! The Church now lives!'

"Throughout the progress of the work the leaders showed a remarkable willingness to follow the lead of the Spirit, even though the sight of physical prostrations, dancing, and wild excitement would have been previously repugnant to them."[14]

Brynmor Jones is even more descriptive in some of the accounts he records of the same revival: "The sober, sedate Calvinistic congregation that gathered in Mount Seion that morning received a shock." It was not their own pastor leading, but Evan Roberts and his "worship team."

"The divine assaults of the Eternal Spirit were seen striking down men like corpses all over the floor...not a few were frightened at the sights they saw.... I know of a man of lukewarm temperament, and of a cold and precise philosophical turn of mind, on the spur of the moment being set ablaze like a bonfire; and all who saw him going wild, clamouring, and bounding like a hart back and forth from the ground floor to the gallery, and from seat to seat through the chapel, thinking that he had for certain taken leave of his senses.... His opinion to this day is that the Spirit of the Lord in a supernatural way was moving him from the narrow circle of his reason, his understanding, and his knowledge, to the wide world of the spiritual."[15]

* * *

---

14. Eifion Evans, *The Welsh Revival of 1904* (Worcester: Evangelical Press of Wales, 1969), 156.
15. Brynmor Jones, *Op. cit.*, 159-160.

"Do You Approve or Disapprove of the Meetings on the Whole?"

Sixty years earlier, revival swept through much of Scotland. One of its leaders was W.C. Burns, of Kilsyth Church. On September 1, 1841, he wrote a letter in which he unguardedly names the discredit and animosity brought against him; the balance of the letter is a description of the work of grace in which he was privileged to play a part:

> "Perhaps you have heard of the wonderful things which the great God has been doing for us in Scotland. The servants of Satan have reviled God's blessed work; and I wish to tell you something of the truth about it. You know that many people come from the church the same way as they went to it; the Word does not touch their consciences, and they remain under the power of sin and Satan, of death and hell. This used to be very much the way among us until lately; but the God of love has visited us, and poured out His life-giving Spirit upon the dead souls of men. In some places you might see the solemn sight of hundreds weeping for their sins, and seeking to give up their hearts to Jesus. And, ah, what a sweet change has taken place on many! The high looks of the proud have been brought down; dead formalists have become living Christians; worshippers of Mammon have been changed into lovers of God; the blasphemous tongues of the profane have been made to sing God's praise...."[16]

Though the local pastor of Kilsyth, Burns also preached itinerantly, and along with other revival leaders, he was mightily used of God in the autumn of 1839. Through his ministry, the Lord graciously ushered in a new season of fervor and awakening in a number of parishes throughout

---

16. William C. Burns, *Revival Sermons* (Edinburgh: The Banner of Truth Trust, 1980), 9.

Scotland. This was so much the case that in December 1840, the Presbytery of Aberdeen appointed a committee to examine reports of the revival that was sweeping the area. They had "concerns," and so issued a questionnaire for their pastors to complete.

While conducting a pastor's conference in Edinburgh, I was handed a copy of this questionnaire, *"Evidence on Revivals: Answers to Queries on the Subject of the Revival of Religion in St. Peter's Parish, Dundee."* The pastor responding was Robert Murray McCheyne. I found the Presbytery's questions and McCheyne's reflections to be most interesting and engaging. McCheyne completed the questionnaire on March 26, 1841, and was commenting on the church's experience over the last 19 months, since August of 1839. When I was given the following account, it was about the same amount of time that had transpired since January 20, 1994, and the beginning of the renewal in Toronto. There is over a 150-year spread between McCheyne's time and ours. So much has changed in a century and a half, yet there is a certain timelessness to the theological and pastoral issues raised by an outpouring of God's Spirit. The following is an abbreviated version of the questionnaire McCheyne was asked to answer. Such extended consideration is given to his responses because it provides considerable insight into how a previous "renewal" unfolded, such that historians speak of the "Scottish Revival of Religion." The concerns and questions, and the reflections and resources brought to bear can serve us as we attempt to discern the renewing and reviving work of the Spirit in our midst, in our day.

By way of context, Robert Murray McCheyne was one of Scotland's bright lights, a leading, respected, and honored pastor. He knew enough Hebrew to be able to converse with European Jews. He read the Greek classics for pleasure, and to keep his journal private, he made his entries in Latin. For the record, McCheyne and his fellow Presbyterians maintained the five classic points of Calvinism: total depravity, unconditional election, limited atonement, irresistible grace, and the perseverance of the saints.

These are the questions to which McCheyne was to respond:

1. "Have revivals taken place in your parish or district; and if so, to what extent, and by what instrumentality and means?"

2-4. These raised issues of the "previous character and habits" of those involved. Have any abandoned their evil practices? (Drunkenness and neglect of family duties and public ordinances are specifically named.) Have any become "remarkable for their diligence in the use of the means of grace?" Has there been recognizable life-change?

5. "Has the conduct of these parties been consistent; and how long has it lasted?"

6. The same questions (2-5) are asked, but corporately considered, not only for the local church, but the surrounding region.

7. "Were there any public manifestations of physical excitement, as in sobs, groans, cries, screams?"

8. "Did any of the parties throw themselves into unusual postures?"

9. "Were there any who fainted, fell into convulsions, or were ill in any other respects?" (It seems that there was some bias against the manifestations!)

10. "How late have you ever known revival meetings to last?" (Understood in the context of a strong Calvinist work ethic, this question makes more sense than it might otherwise. Is it likely to be God at work if those "revived" are up so late the night before that they're no good for work come the next morning?)

11. "Do you approve or disapprove of the meetings upon the whole? In either case, have the goodness to state why."

12. "Was any death occasioned, or said to be occasioned, by overexcitement, in any such case? If so, state the circumstances, insofar as you know them." (The issue here is the attempt to bring clarity to exaggerated and distorted reports of the meetings.)

13. "State any other circumstances connected with revivals in your parish or district, which, though not involved in the foregoing queries, may tend to throw light upon the subject."

Mr. McCheyne answers as follows:

1. On revival: "It is my decided and solemn conviction that a very remarkable and glorious work of God, in the conversion of sinners and edifying of saints, has taken place in this parish and neighbourhood." He had begun his ministry in that parish in November 1836, four years earlier, and while there had been "evident blessing from on high in many instances," "there was no visible movement among the people until August 1839, when the Word of God came with such power to the hearts and consciences of the people, and their thirst for hearing it became so intense, that the evening classes in the schoolroom were changed into densely crowded congregations in the church" that gathered together for worship almost every night for four months. Thirty-nine "house groups" also began during this period, five of which were "conducted and attended entirely by little children." He names several visiting ministers who assisted in the work; McCheyne says, "I have good reason for believing that they were eminently countenanced by God in their labours."

"As to the extent of this work of God, I believe it is impossible to speak decidedly." He notes that people came from "all quarters of the town," from "all ranks and denominations of people." "I am deeply persuaded, the number of those who have received saving benefit is greater than anyone will know till the judgement day."

2-3. On life-change: "...Not a few have become new creatures." "Many, again, who were before nominal Christians are now living ones." Some were radically converted from "paths of open sin." He names the power of a credible witness: "I often think, when conversing with some of these, that the change they have undergone might be enough to convince an atheist that there is a God, or an infidel that there is a Saviour."

4. On numbers: McCheyne recognizes that it's impossible to keep an exact account of all "awakening or conversion; and there are many of which the minister may never hear." He does state that in the autumn of 1839, not fewer than 600 to 700 "came to converse with the ministers about their souls."

5. On conduct and consistency: "Many who came under concern for their souls have gone back to the world." But in that "remarkable season in 1839, there were very few persons who attended the meetings without being more or less affected. But many allowed it to slip past them without being saved...and alas! There are some among us, whose very looks remind you of that awful warning, 'Quench not the Spirit.' "

McCheyne knows of only two who "have openly given the lie to their profession." But "many there are among us, who are filled with light and peace and are examples to believers in all things."

McCheyne describes extra communion services held as the "happiest and holiest" he ever attended. The entire day was spent in thanksgiving and a special offering was generously given, and sent to missions.[17]

6. On regional influence: McCheyne reflects that, sadly, the majority in Dundee remain unmoved, "still sunk in deep apathy in regard to spiritual things, or are running on greedily in open sin."

But he names special favor from the Lord to establish 19 Sabbath schools, all of which were well taught and well attended. Previously, these had been impossible to institute. (The issue of special favor will feature prominently in future considerations.)

7-9. On public manifestations: "There were many seasons of remarkable solemnity, when the house of God became literally a 'Bochim, a place of weepers.' Those who have been present at the meetings, I believe, never will forget them.... I have seen the preaching of the Word attended with so much power, and eternal things brought so near, that the feelings of the people could not be restrained." He says there have been times of "awful and breathless stillness," "half-suppressed sighs," "many bathed in tears," "a loud sobbing." Some, "cried aloud, as if pierced through with a dart." All of that was *during the preaching*.

But it's not *just* tears of repentance that characterized the meetings.

McCheyne continues, "I have seen persons so overcome, that they could not walk or stand alone. I have known cases in which believers have been similarly affected through the fullness of their joy...." He concludes his comments of the manifestations with a call for discernment: "I am far from believing that these signs always issue in conversion, or that the Spirit of God does not often work in a more quiet manner. Sometimes, I believe, He comes like the pouring rain; sometimes like the gentle dew."

---

17. The themes of gratitude, generosity, and mission are recurrent in true revival.

10-11. How late do the revival meetings go, and do you approve?

(Note McCheyne's response to naming things "revival.") "None of the ministers who have been engaged in the work of God here have ever used the name *revival* meeting; nor do they approve of its use. We are told in the Acts that the apostles preached and taught the gospel daily; yet their meetings are never called revival meetings."

As to the meetings, they usually went to ten o'clock. Sometimes, there was such a move of the Spirit, they had to stay longer, so many sought prayer—sometimes till midnight.

"On such occasions I have longed that all the ministers in Scotland were present, that they might learn more deeply what the true end of our ministry is…. The feelings that fill my soul are those of the most solemn awe, the deepest compassion for afflicted souls, and an unutterable sense of the hardness of my own heart. I do entirely and solemnly approve of such meetings…and it is my earnest prayer that we may yet see greater things than these in all parts of Scotland."

12. Any deaths? Yes, but the report on the thing was maliciously distorted, "A groundless calumny."

13. There was space on the questionnaire for further reflections. As many of us have done in the midst of this current outpouring, McCheyne studied previous revivals in order to understand what he was experiencing. He reviewed the historical records of other revivals in Scotland and the Great Awakening in America and concluded: "The outpouring of the Holy Spirit…was attended by the very same appearances as the work in our own day. Indeed, so completely do they seem to agree, both in their nature and the circumstances that attended them, I have not heard a single objection brought against the work of God now

which was not urged against in former times, and has not been most scripturally and triumphantly removed by President Edwards in his invaluable *Thoughts Concerning the Present Revival, and the ways in which it is to be acknowledged and promoted.*"

McCheyne then quotes Edwards: "And certainly we must throw by all talk of conversion and Christian experience; and not only so, but we must throw by our Bibles, and give up revealed religion, if this be not in general the work of God."[18]

Exponential Consequences

As God renews and revives His people in these special seasons of grace, it is as if the wind of His Spirit ripples the pond. The effects of His powerful presence are felt in ever widening circles of influence, often beginning with pastoral leadership, then throughout local congregations, and then beyond the walls of the church.

As to how this is felt out on the edge, there is a telling anecdote of a conversation that took place between the circuit riding Methodist preacher, Francis Asbury, and a young man, roughly 220 years ago. The young man approached Asbury and said, "Heard you were at the Methodist meeting." "Sure was," came the reply. "Any shouting?" "Some." "Why do Methodists shout?" "Because they're happy." "Well," replied the young man, "I can't see how anyone could be happy in church. Whenever I go I feel like a corpse."[19]

As the dialogue song between the shouting Methodist and the Formalist made so delightfully clear, revival typically

18. Andrew Bonar, ed., *Memories of McCheyne, II: Messages and Miscellaneous Papers.* (Chicago: Moody Press), 221-231.
19. Charles Ludwig, *Francis Asbury: God's Circuit Rider* (Milford, Michigan: Mott Media, 1984), 1.

begins with the reviving of the preacher. As McCheyne's re-flections indicate, the next to be revived is the local church. Though unsettling to many, the physical manifestations that so characteristically accompany an outpouring of God's Spirit play an important role in taking things further.

What Draws the Unsaved?

One of the ways to understand the physical manifesta-tions that often accompany a reviving work of the Holy Spirit is that they serve as God's own advertising. To change the metaphor, they are like fisherman's bait. A bare hook in the water generates little by way of interest; what's needed is something on there that draws some attention. In the midst of all that's taking place in revival meetings, it is the physical manifestations that generate a significant amount of attention!

To look at things another way, consider the following: why did unbelievers come out to hear Wesley preach? Because they woke up one morning and figured they had bet-ter go get saved? At least as Wesley records in his *Journals*, some were drawn for other reasons:

> "*Curiosity* led [a young woman from London] to hear a sermon, which cut her to the heart. One standing by, ob-served how she was affected, and took occasion to talk with her. The two corresponded by letter; the first was told, 'Christ is ready to receive you: Now is the day of sal-vation.' Quickened, she responded, 'It is! It is! Christ is mine!' and was filled with joy unspeakable."[20]

The phrase, "they came, either to hear or see" recurs in Wesley's daily entries, as in the following account:

20. John Wesley, *Journals* (Grand Rapids, Michigan: Baker Book House, 1984), 453. Entry from Feb. 17, 1772. Italics added.

"Edward Farles had been an hearer for many years, but
was never convinced of sin. Hearing that there was much
roaring and crying at the prayer-meetings, he came to hear
and see for himself. That evening many cried to God for
mercy. He said himself he wished it was all real; and went
away more prejudiced than before, especially against the
roarers and criers, as he called them. But soon after he got
home, he was struck to the ground, so distressed that he
was convulsed all over. His family, fearing that he would
die, sent for some of the praying people. For some hours
he seemed to be every moment on the point of expir-
ing...but, about four in the morning, God in a moment
healed both soul and body. Ever since he has adorned the
Gospel."[21]

In his classic work, *Revival*, Martyn Lloyd Jones reminds
his readers that if revival broke out in the church, "the man
in the street, and all his friends would come in."

Why? Quite simply: "He comes because he has suddenly
heard that something strange and wonderful is happening
in that church.... The man in the street is only attracted finally by power."[22]

Jones then cites Acts 2:12-13, "They were all amazed and
perplexed, saying to one another, 'What can this mean?'
Others said contemptuously, 'They have been drinking!' "
By way of comment, he candidly reflects on the characteristic ways in which unusual phenomena accompany a revival of religion:

"There are people, who dismiss, and denounce, the whole
notion of revival because of these phenomena, and therefore when they are exhorted to pray for revival, they say,

---

21. *Ibid.*, June 5, 1772: 471. See also December 21, 1776: 90.
22. Martyn Lloyd Jones, *Revival* (Wheaton, Illinois: Crossway Books,
    1994), 61-62.

'Most certainly not. We do not want that sort of thing. We
are not interested in that kind of experience.' And, thus,
without realizing it, they are often guilty of quenching the
Spirit.'"[23]

Brynmor Jones, in *Voices From the Welsh Revival 1904-1905*
traces similar dynamics, when he comments that:

"the strange coldness and passiveness of the [visiting]
ministers, content to remain mere observers, robbed them
of the blessing.... The powerful emotional upheavals of
this kind did not go down well with all the ministers and
church leaders.... [Nevertheless], people came for very
mixed reasons and even the most distinguished visitors
confessed to new experiences. Many came originally to
watch events but were consequently caught up in them....
No one had seen meetings of this kind before and it is little
wonder that the many visitors were fascinated. One can
share the feelings of that aged man who called out, 'I came
three thousand miles to this meeting, but I would go round
the world to see such as this.'

"The consequence [of the revival within] the Church is
that it is made attractive to the world. People cannot help
going to church or chapel now. Sensible men, though they
may be unsympathetic, talk respectfully about the Church
of Christ today. Moreover the Church is aggressive. Awakened itself to its own needs, it has at the same time been
awakened to the needs of the unconverted and unregener-
ate world outside. It can be said of the Church of
Wales...that great grace is upon all. There is the grace of
love and compassion."[24]

23. *Ibid.*, 136.
24. Brynmor Jones, *Op. cit.*, 79, 114, 116, 155, 200.

Open Doors

In terms of a characteristic process of revival, what seems to take place is that first and foremost, the Lord graciously renews, refreshes, and releases leadership; their influence, in turn, brings transformation to local congregations. The renewed, even revived church moves outside of herself with new passion, vision, confidence, boldness, and authority to share the love of Jesus. Combined with a sensed "season of favor" initiated by the Lord Himself, spiritual doors swing wide open as never before.

This has repeatedly been the case in our present experience. On May 24, 1995, seven of us were invited to be the featured guests of the Phil Donahue Show, one of the leading North American daytime TV talk shows.[25] Characteristically, Donahue has not been particularly interested in the Church of Jesus Christ. The few times he has had Christian leaders on the show, he has been caustic, accusatory, and faultfinding. The only reason Donahue was interested in us at all was because of the reports of hysterical laughter. The physical manifestations continue to prove to be provocative, so much so that he extended to us the invitation to talk about our experience on prime-time television.

We spent a great deal of time praying about the invitation, and felt that the Lord had opened a significant door for us, so we accepted. We were able to go with wonderful freedom, in part, because we realized that the Lord had called us to be His witnesses, not His lawyers. We would share what we had experienced of the power of our heavenly Father's love and grace, and leave things at that.

With incredulity, Donahue read from various headlines: *The Toronto Star*: "Laughing all the way to Heaven." *Florida Today*: "Floored by God." Another, "Church that has them

---

25. The show aired September 19, 1995.

rolling in the aisles." *Christian Week*: "Toronto Blessing garnering worldwide attention." Another: "Holy high jinx: thousands flock to church that's just for laughs." It was the manifestations, especially the laughter, that held Donahue's interest, and that, because it was so very far outside of his own experience in church. As he turned to my wife, the first person he interviewed, he asked, "Janis Chevreau, you believe this is God manifesting Himself through the people in attendance. Do I understand you?"

For 51 minutes, the seven of us got to talk about the grace of God, the love of the Lord Jesus Christ, and the powerful presence of the Holy Spirit, before a viewing audience of 13 million people. That's the largest congregation any of us had ever preached to! And because of very favorable audience response, the show has been re-televised repeatedly.

The New Life team of the Toronto Airport Christian Fellowship knows when the show has re-aired, because when they ask the newly saved why they have come forward for prayer, the answer comes: "I saw you guys on the Donahue show, and I had to see if it was for real."

One man from Michigan, for instance, watched the rerun in June of 1996. He was so moved by what he saw of the supernatural power of God, he said to his wife, "I just have to go to that church this Sunday." He made a four hour drive to Toronto, and responded to the altar call at the end of the Sunday morning service. With tears streaming down his face, he surrendered his life to Jesus.[26]

Urban Rebirth

As the wind of the Spirit continues to blow, the pond's ripples move further and further out. Not only are individuals

---

26. As reported by John Arnott, *Spread the Fire* vol. 2, no. 4, Aug. 1996: 2.

converted, the grace of God redeems and revives whole communities.

In May 1995, Vineyard pastor and overseer Steve Phillips was invited to speak at Bethesda Full Gospel Church in Buffalo, New York. This is an inner city, predominantly black congregation of about 900 members led by Pastor Michael Badger. Many from the church had been attending meetings at the Toronto Airport Christian Fellowship since the early days of the renewal. Steve has preached several times at TACF, and without knowing it, had prayed for a number of this congregation while ministering in Toronto.

When he was at Bethesda, one young man named Melvin Taylor asked him if he remembered the prophetic words he had given to him in Toronto. The word Steve had spoken to Melvin was that God was going to use him to raise up gangs of people to go through the city doing spiritual drive-bys, "shooting" prayers of blessing at those walking and standing on the streets. Further, the Lord would be sending him to the street corners of the nations to proclaim His Word, such that revival would come through the inner cities.

Melvin had received a similar word prior to Steve's from Grace Lee, of Woman's Aglow. Upon hearing it again, Melvin decided it was time to get on with it!

What Melvin did not know was that the youth pastor, Kenny Williams, had received a word that he was to cancel the weekly youth meetings, and begin weekly "drive-by" prayer attacks in a very crime-ridden neighborhood nearby. At first he thought this could not be God. "The church will never put up with this!" he reasoned. But the leading would not go away, so he arrived at church one night ready to announce this new plan to the youth group when he noticed the choir practicing on stage. Immediately, he felt God say, "Go tell the choir director that he is supposed to cancel practice and take the choir in the lead cars like the tribe of Judah leading Israel around Jericho!" Kenny had little faith for a favorable response. He was surprised, therefore, when the choir director simply said, "All right, I will."

For several weeks they drove around the neighborhood, singing praises and praying as they passed gang members on the street. Several times they saw the Spirit of God move significantly as people would come over to the cars to talk with them. On one occasion a young man wept as he accepted Christ. He then displayed the gun he had under his coat. He said that he was on his way to kill someone.

During all this time, Melvin was unaware of Kenny's street worship and prayer activity. On his own, he was planning to do a tent meeting in a neighborhood that was known for its gunfire, prostitution, and heavy drug traffic. Without any money except his pastor's support, Melvin ordered the tent and wrote checks for all of the necessary equipment and began the "Possessing the Land" meetings that ran from July 17th until September 3rd, 49 days in total. On the third day of the crusade, one of the checks bounced.

The person who sold Melvin the tent was very upset, and threatened to repossess his merchandise. Melvin assured him that the funds were forthcoming. At the conclusion of their business negotiations, Melvin got on his knees. By the time he'd finished praying, calls of support and financial assistance began coming from numerous sources.

The meetings were blessed by a powerful outpouring of the Father's presence. Some 400 people responded to the Lord's call. The churches from the city began to support the meetings.[27]

---

27. Melvin can be reached by fax at 716-884-3595.

From the time the tent was set up, there were no reports of shooting or murders in the ten-block, three-avenue perimeter that was sealed off by the prayer walks and the drive-by blessings. One year before, 50 murders were committed in that area. In a television interview, the police commissioner stated that "for some reason that he was not sure of," the neighborhood's crime rate had dropped 33 percent compared to the previous year. There had been significant drug busts; key drug dealers had been arrested; and many crack houses were shut down.

When Melvin returned to the neighborhood recently, local shopkeepers and community people came to express their gratitude and support for what Melvin had started the year before. Many of them reported that the neighborhood was a completely different place, and that their business profits were significantly increased, up from the previous year. They were also quick to add that their stores had not been robbed since the meetings.

I asked Steve Phillips to reflect on his experience at Bethesda. He commented:

"In Ezekiel 36:33, God says, 'On that day I will cleanse you from all your iniquities, I will also enable you to dwell in the cities and the ruins will be rebuilt.' Perhaps we presumptuously believe that we know what it takes to build a society and live together. It's just possible that the destruction of our cities is an outgrowth of that presumption. It may be that we will not see the problems of crime, violence and drugs solved until we, in humility, ask the Father to cleanse us and 'enable us' to dwell in the cities. I believe Michael Badger's congregation is a shining example of this model of spiritual, urban rebirth and revival."

* * *

Monday is the only night of the week when there is no evening meeting at the Toronto Airport Christian Fellowship. Consequently, many out-of-town visitors rent a car and

drive around Lake Ontario to Niagara Falls. Those who do
so in the month of May are awed, not only by the grandeur
of the mighty Niagara, but also the acres and acres of blos-
soming fruit trees along the highway.

Blossoms are a good way of thinking about the physical
manifestations and the wonderful work that the Spirit of
God is doing in our midst. The fruit trees on the Niagara Es-
carpment are not planted and cared for in order to produce
blossoms, as beautiful as they are. It is as St. Augustine commented on John 15:6: *Aut vitus, aut ignis*. Freely translated,
it's "fruit, or firewood." May's blossoms are at best signals,
pointers, the "manifestations," of a larger, longer dynamic
at work. What is taking place is an "impartation" of sap that,
under proper conditions, yields September's fruit-bearing.

There are many people who come to relish the beauty of
the blossoms, in and of themselves. But there are many
more who come months later to pick their own fruit. Many
more still eat of the harvest, without ever seeing the blossoms that "advertised" the wonderful season of new growth
that had been initiated months earlier.

The balance of *Share the Fire* is a consideration of the
evangelistic fruit that our Lord purposes us to bear as we
abide in Him and His words dwell in us.[28]

---

28. John 15:7.

Chapter 3

Church Growth, Renewal, and Grace-Based Evangelism:

A Confession

...You and we belong to Christ, guaranteed as His and anointed, it is all God's doing; it is God also who has set His seal upon us and, as a pledge of what is to come, has given the Spirit to dwell in our hearts (2 Corinthians 1:21-22).

* * *

My doctoral thesis was titled *A Pastoral Explication of John Calvin's Instruction on Private Prayer.* It represented the culmination of a six-year study of 16 centuries of God's renewing, reviving work in His Church. Upon its completion, I needed to catch up with what was currently happening and so devoted myself to the study of Church growth literature, a very different world from the historical and theological research I had done previously. Nevertheless, I found the field engaging, and read widely.[1] Following many of the

---

1. A partial list of titles is indicative of some of the themes considered: *Where Do We Go From Here; Activating the Passive Church; The Church on Purpose; Prepare Your Church for the Future; Growing a Healthy Church; Twelve Keys to an Effective Church; Marketing the Church; Leading Your Church to Growth; Leading and Managing Your Church; Mastering Church Management; Management of Ministry; Managing the Non-Profit Organization.*

footnotes to their sources, I read some of the current business literature as complement.[2]

I also spent my study leaves at various church growth conferences. Among other places, I went to Willowcreek Community Church in North Barrington, Chicago. From the senior pastor, Bill Hybels, I "caught" some of their evangelistic passion for those whom they have affectionately called "unchurched Harry and Mary."

All of this study clarified my thinking, sharpened my vision, and taught me a lot about evangelism, leadership, and the ministry of the local church. It was the resource pool from which we drew as we articulated the mission philosophy and mandate for the church we were attempting to plant in the fall of 1993.

Without diminishing or dishonoring the value of things learned in formal study, eclectic reading, and time spent at Willowcreek and other Church growth conferences, the "Toronto Blessing" has made it clear to me that it is not so much what is taught, or caught, that makes the transformative difference in a church's life and mission; it is what is *given*.

Reaching the Unchurched

In the very early 1990's, one of my friends relayed the following story to me. At the time, he was the senior pastor of a "significant" university church. After their annual report was reviewed, he was asked, "Pastor, have I missed something? There doesn't seem to be an evangelism committee here at this church; is that under the mandate of the

2. *Teaching the Elephant to Dance; Thriving on Chaos; Running Through Walls; Barbarians to Bureaucrats; Leaders; Becoming a Leader; The Visionary Leader; Leadership and the One Minute Manager; The Art of Leadership; Servant Leadership; Principle-Centered Leadership; Why Leaders Can't Lead; The Leadership Secrets of Attila the Hun.*

missions commission?" He responded, "No...evangelism is really the mandate of the entire church...." " There followed a pregnant pause, the "oh-oh...." kind. *"Evangelism is really the mandate of the entire church...."*

My pastor friend confessed ZERO conversion growth that particular year. I felt as chagrined as he did. Our net conversion growth for that year had been 2.3 percent, but those two couples were our "harvest" after six years of ministry.

At the time, my pastor friend and I were working through the rather depressing book, *Fragmented Gods: The Poverty and Potential of Religion in Canada.* In it, Bibby cites the growth studies he conducted of evangelistic churches in Calgary, a Canadian city demographically similar to the one in which I was living at the time. In findings he titled, "The Circulation of the Saints," Bibby stated that the net conversion growth for the surveyed churches was 1.9 percent.[3] Given the fact that I had been preaching, I felt, passionately, "The Church exists for those who are not yet a part of it," and that "we in Christ are God's missionary people," and that, indeed, "evangelism is the mandate of the entire church," it was small comfort that we were ahead of the Calgary average by 0.4 percent for *that* particular year. We were pathetically below average if previous years were factored into the equation.

So convinced was I of the primacy of evangelism that I resigned the traditional church I had been pastoring and devoted myself to planting a church where I would be working with those similarly devoted to an uncompromised commitment to reaching the unchurched. In Oakville, the community to which we moved, well over 90 percent of the

---

3. Reginald Bibby, "The Circulation of the Saints," *Fragmented Gods: The Poverty and Potential of Religion in Canada* (Toronto: Irwin Publishing, 1987), 30.

people we surveyed believed in God. We had to hold a rather open definition. Some believed their *cat* was God. Nevertheless, over 90 percent believed in something more than themselves, something more than the material world. They believed in something of transcendence. However, only 4 percent of Oakville were in church on a Sunday. One could rightly draw a quick conclusion: "God, yes; church, no."

On the home front, the book *Cinderella* was one of my daughter's favorites. We read and reread it together. One night, as I was looking out the window, the glass slipper scene clarified what I knew intuitively. If traditional churches were meeting the needs of the 90 percent who believed in God, they would be in church. If things were the right size and shape and style, it would be a wonderful "fit." But by their not being in church, it was an indication that for all sorts of folks, the traditional "glass slipper" did not fit.

Our mission mandate became crystal clear: we were "in business" (I was reading a lot of business management material) because we recognized that there were a whole lot of folk in Oakville who would never fit the traditional glass slipper, as beautiful and precious and formative as that slipper was for many. We were "segmenting the market," knowing that there are a whole lot of people who have been raised wearing Nike running shoes, folks who would NEVER fit the slipper.

Organized to Death

With a well-researched, carefully crafted, and illustrated mission philosophy in hand, we knew what our vision was; we had clear goals and guiding principles; and we had a magnificent five-year plan.

Our core mission value was declared simply enough: we were committed to "intentional relational evangelism." Strategically, we taught the maxim: "Figure out what you love doing, and go do it with the unchurched." To model it, my co-pastor, Kim, and I went down to the local yacht club and asked if there were any skippers looking for crew. A few days later we received a call from Bill.[4] He had just bought a new boat and wanted to race Tuesday nights. Were we interested? Were we interested?!

For the next several Tuesdays, we had an exhilarating time aboard a 36 footer, with seven other unchurched guys. Kim and I were doing a great job "intentionally relating." We'd race for an hour and a half and then spend three hours shooting the breeze. During that time, we heard non-stop bravado, conquest, and testosterone. After five weeks, the skipper finally got round to Kim and me and asked, "What do you guys do for a living?" When we answered, "We're pastors," their faces went blank as they rewound the tapes of the previous five weeks' conversations....

I developed a good relationship with Bill, and we got along swimmingly as long as we related as one entrepreneur to another. But any time I tried to shift the conversation to "spiritual things," the conversation ran aground and became forced. That was painfully the case when I tried the "Bill, if you were to die tonight..." question.

Let the reader understand: Bill is the most successful businessman I know. He is the most intelligent, synthetic, global, trans-national thinker I have ever been privileged to meet. One could very easily, and correctly, conclude that he has the world by the tail, and that he owns a significant part of it—tax-free.

"Bill, if you were to die tonight...." He sent non-verbals that indicated that he thought the question was beneath both our dignity. He answered, "I'm not going to. Die. Tonight." And that was the end of that. We changed the subject of conversation to spinnakers and depth-sounders.

---

4. His name has been changed.

Ancient Scripts

Along with the Church growth literature I had read, there was a sideline study: burnout. It has little to do with the length of time one works. We can find ourselves burned out working 30 hours a week. Burnout is the malaise that leaves us miserable day after day, week after week, month after tedious month. Physiologically, its symptoms include difficulty in sleeping, weight loss or gain, headaches, backaches, and intestinal problems. Emotionally, burnout is characterized by chronic tiredness and irritability, low-grade to desperate depression and nagging boredom.

At the forefront is a crisis of expectations. There rises up a systemic disappointment as expectations exceed experience. "The best laid plans of mice and men...." In the pastorate, most have high hopes to see the church grow. With that hope, there are diverse and contradicting congregational expectations as to the conduct of a pastor's ministry, such that no pastor can possibly meet them all. Regardless of what he or she does, it will not be right in somebody's estimation, and they'll more than likely say so—to someone else.

Especially as a church planter, I found myself attempting to function with both a chronic shortage of resources and a pervasive sense of inadequacy. Together, they acted catalytically to generate full-blown despair, and with it, a fatigue and sense of frustration, even failure. Things kept erupting into not-so-occasional outbursts of rage. When those firestorms had settled, the climate was one of a deep loneliness.

Much of the literature suggests solutions to burnout that encourage one to manage time more effectively. Again, there are some great books that are invaluable resources.[5]

---

5. *The One Minute Manager; The Time Trap; Time Power; Seven Habits of Highly Effective People;* and *First Things First.*

When surveyed and distilled, the common denominator of the time management literature is strategic goal setting and prioritization. Thoreau put the issue dynamically: "For every thousand hacking at the leaves of evil, there is one hacking at the roots." Instead of attending to symptoms, address the causes. The thing was, I *had* a carefully crafted personal *and* corporate mission statement. I understood that it was "value-driven work" that yielded the highest dividends. The "driven" bit, however, I always found unsettling. It seemed to stir some deeply imbedded scripts down in wherever scripts are embedded. I could almost see the clipped comments, in red, on the side bars of my childhood report cards: "Can do better." "Guy fails to apply himself."

Especially in the context of the church plant, my performance orientation was in full bloom. I was suffering from acute "results anxiety," especially with respect to evangelism. Like a hungry, commission-driven salesman, I was trying to close the deal; the response I was getting was, "Just browsing; killing time." Even if it was eternally.

Illusory Reprieve

In the burnout literature, some of the things that came highly recommended were spiritual retreats, keeping a journal, and regular recreational activity. Come freeze-up and the end of the year's sailing, what I did to "recreate" was devote an hour of my Tuesday evenings to the TV show, *MacGyver*. Every week, MacGyver would get himself into an impossible situation, and against incredible odds, extricate himself using whatever he could find at hand, along with his ever-present roll of duct tape and his Swiss Army knife. My favorite episode saw him deep in Central America; his mission: to rescue a captured American agent. She was being held prisoner by subversive guerrillas. He sneaks in and finds her, gets her out of prison and, with an old tarpaulin and some bamboo, makes a hang glider. While machine guns are blazing away and bombs are going off, the two of them leap from a nearby cliff, and soar to safety.

MacGyver's ingenuity and tenacity served me well in the midst of my burnout. Not only was it a great mental break, it was highly inspirational. No matter how desperate the situation, he would never give up. When I would run aground doing whatever it was I was trying to do, I would look out the window and ask myself, "What would MacGyver do in this situation?"

The trouble was, my gummy roll of duct tape and fancy Swiss Army knife were not enough to see me through. The "hang glider" that I built did not fly. We jumped off the cliff, and my "intentional relational evangelism" and the church plant we so carefully and creatively constructed not only did not carry us, it crashed pitifully, and we barely escaped the wreckage.

Reflecting on things at length, I realized something that I never read in the literature. Burnout is rooted in bitterness. Anytime we commit ourselves to a cause, however noble it may be, we will end up frustrated. The reason is that we do not have the resources necessary to see a noble cause through to its fulfillment. Over time, this frustration becomes bitterness, and this bitterness poisons us to the core. I found it a sobering coincidence that ten days before we went to our first meeting at the Toronto Airport Vineyard, February 1, 1994, my kidneys were on the verge of failure. I very nearly died of systemic septicemia, the medical name for full-blown blood poisoning. Upon my doctor's examination, I had no externally infected sight. He was quite puzzled, as there was no determinable source to the infection that raged within my body. I knew better.

I had become so frustrated because I knew that I did not have what I needed to see our church plant "cause" through to fulfillment. Again, our carefully crafted mission philosophy stated that we were committed to "intentional relational evangelism." Mine was forced and driven. Though I truly enjoyed the friendships with the unchurched that I was making, my faith-sharing was not motivated by a heart-compassion for my friends who did not yet know how much God loved them. Rather, if I am honest enough, it was fuelled by my need to succeed, to demonstrate to the core group, the support churches, my denominational executives, other clergy colleagues, and anyone else who was even mildly interested, that my ministry was viable. I needed my new friends' conversions to show in hard numbers that I was able to evangelize and grow a church.

Our mission goal was "conversion growth of 60 percent, to be assessed semi-annually." But my coworker and I had to develop a way of ducking the "How big's your church?" competition. Our answer: "Something under a thousand." In actual fact, our weekly attendance was somewhere in the twenties, more or less. Numbers alone do not tell the whole tale: our growth curve was taking a nosedive. We were losing core members fast.

That's why MacGyver was so recreationally distracting. While I was exploring the landscape of failure, I would live vicariously his success vistas. If only I, too, could snoop around in the cupboard, or attic, or laundry room, in the workshop, the garden house, the junk yard—and come up with whatever was needed. Oh, to be like MacGyver—no matter what the situation, he was infinitely resourceful, and resourced.

It was such a short reprieve. Come 9:00 p.m. every Tuesday night, I would again be face-to-face with my existential bankruptcy. For all my carefully strategized, prioritized, and consecrated intentions, things were just about over. I was mad at myself, and mad at those who were supposed to be working with me. I was mad at God for not seeing His end through. And the Church growth gurus' inspirations were not motivating any longer: "The greatest barriers to church planting are in the mind. Once we make up our mind to do it, it can be done."[6] I *had* made up my mind; the thing was, a hand had appeared, and I could read the handwriting on the wall: *Mene mene tekel upharsin*—"Weighed in the balance and found wanting."[7]

Up by Our Bootstraps?

I should have known better. Motivated by a strong (stubborn) will, I had unwittingly embraced a pragmatic Pelagianism. Pelagius was a priest who lived in the latter part of the fourth century and early decades of the fifth. He taught a self-confidence, specifically with respect to personal holiness. Within his lifetime, his teachings were condemned as heresy, for they were essentially salvation by works, an overstatement of human freedom and the power of choice. As the unrecognized father of "self-actualization," he gave no recognition to human limitations.

One of the Doctors of the Church, Augustine of Hippo, countered Pelagius. In a treatise titled *On Faith, Hope, and Love*, he refutes Pelagianism at length. With optimistically gritted teeth, Pelagius argued, "My liberty is such that I can do all things." Augustine responds, "Your freedom accomplishes nothing without God. It depends on Him in everything, for everything. The only thing you have that's all your own is your sin. That you can manage all by yourself, without God's help."[8] Augustine understood Pelagian self-determination as the very root of sin—and the very

---

6. C. Peter Wagner, *Church Planting for a Greater Harvest* (Ventura, California: Regal Books, 1990), 27.

7. Daniel 5:25-28.

8. See Augustine's *Enchiridion*, Nicene and Post-Nicene Fathers, III. Philip Shaff, ed. (Peabody, Massachusetts: Hendrickson Publishers, 1994), 247.

denial of salvation in Christ. Rather than our attempts to ascend to spiritual heights, God's grace descends to us in Christ. Augustine frequently quoted First Corinthians 1:30: "By God's act you are in Christ Jesus; God has made Him our...righteousness, our holiness, our liberation." Again he says, "The Son of God came that...He might enable us who were the sons of men to become the sons of God...that we might become partakers of His own nature."

Working from Romans 9:16, "[God's promise] does not depend on human will or effort, but on God's mercy," Augustine continues:

> "The whole work belongs to God, who both makes the will of man righteous, and thus prepares it for assistance, and assists it when it is prepared.... [His mercy] goes before the unwilling to make him willing; it follows him willing, that he may not will in vain."[9]

Augustine's prayers, even more than his treatises, so convey the contrast to a self-willed determinism:

> "Let me know You, You who know me; let me know You, as I am known. You are the strength of my soul; enter into it, and prepare it for Yourself, that You may have and hold it without 'spot or wrinkle.' This is my hope...and in this hope do I rejoice...."

> "Too late did I love You, O Beauty, so ancient, and yet so new! Too late did I love You! For behold, You were within, and I without, and there did I seek You; I unlovely, rushed heedlessly among the things of beauty You have made. You were with me, but I was not with You.... You called, and cried aloud, and forced open my deafness. You did gleam and shine, and chase away my blindness. You shed Your fragrance about me; I drew breath and now I pant after You. I tasted, and now I hunger and thirst for

---

9. *Ibid.*, 248.

You. You burned in me the fire of Your love, and I am inflamed with love of Your peace."[10]

Rereading Augustine's *Confessions* called forth my own. Exercising all the will I could muster, I had embraced a "proactive self-directedness" with the best of intentions. Committed to Church growth and evangelism, I had "made up my mind" to go out and do it. As I am a continuous learner, I submitted to those who were "doing it," to the point of giving serious consideration to the counsel of one of my Church growth mentors who said, "In terms of leading the church, my MBA (Master of Business Administration) is of greater value than my MDiv (Master of Divinity)."

What I encountered at the Toronto Airport Vineyard was a counterpoint, a complete pendulum swing. I found grace. Better, *grace found me.*

And that is the gospel of Jesus Christ. As I have travelled around the world these last two and a half years and addressed pastors and leaders from the broadest of denominational cross sections, there is this common denominator to the testimonies: the vast majority have embraced a cause of one form or another. They are devoting their time, energy, and resources to seeing a particular end through to fulfillment, with or without a five-year plan. If candid, and most are, they declare openly that they are facing a measure of burnout and personal bankruptcy.

Coming to a "Catch the Fire" conference is, for many of them, like calling the emergency services. During the call to prayer ministry, someone hears their cry for help. Many have been suffering a spiritual angina for years; some pastors

---

10. Augustine, *Confessions*, XX. 1 and 27, Nicene and Post-Nicene Fathers, I. Philip Schaff, ed. (Peabody, Massachusetts: Hendrickson Publishers, 1994), 142, 152. The syntax has been modernized for ease of reading.

have come with very serious "chest" pains. And some have had the electroshock paddles put to them. With a powerful jolt, life surges into their bodies and spirits, and they feel as if they have been given another ten years.

One of the things I have discovered is that just as with heart attack victims, so it is with spiritually "zapped" and revived people. There are some who nearly immediately return to their old, driven ways. I more than understand. That is the way I am naturally inclined. I love to control, direct, and lead. Those who know and love me call it my inclination to "strive, drive, and connive." I thoroughly enjoyed the energy, the synergy, the adrenaline rush that comes from "closing the deal," be it in terms of making proposals to denominational executives, or securing funding, or property, or recruiting staff. I love the creativity and independent achievement of the entrepreneur. In fact, an "entrepreneurial spirit" was near the top of the list for "Characteristics of Successful Church Planters," and on my profile test, it was my highest score. I had appropriated the key leadership principle that states "leadership takes responsibility." I interpreted this to mean that if anything was going to happen, it was up to me to MAKE it happen.

Past tense. Understood. There are some heart attack victims who undergo a radical life change. Getting "zapped" comes as an "awakening." It is the wake-up call of wake-up calls. There is a complete reevaluation of what is left of life, and a revision of priorities and commitments, a restatement of purpose and life orientation. Characteristically, the drivenness is transformed into gratitude. There is the recognition that life *could* have been over, finished, done. But then there has come "re-vival." Thereafter, every day, is a gift—a bonus. Some folks quite literally start stopping and smelling the roses. I know I do.

Leadership does take responsibility, but responsibility is the "ability to respond." I had been trying to initiate so much, I had way outstepped myself. In terms of church growth, and especially evangelism, this has such profound consequences. The next two chapters ground a revived life in the initiative that God takes. With that foundation firmly established, we can then consider the response that is appropriately ours in Christ.

Chapter 4

Graced to Bless:

A Study in the Acts of the Apostles

*May the Lord direct your hearts towards God's love and the
steadfastness of Christ* (2 Thessalonians 3:5).

* * *

The "Toronto Blessing" has been provocative. While
there is much that should stay on the margins, there are
other dynamics that cause us to think, yet again, about the
core fundamentals of faith. Grace is one of those essentials.
Over the past months, I have been pulling off the shelves
book after book, seeking to enlarge and deepen my understanding of the grace of God.

I began by reviewing some of my theological training. At
seminary, our systematics text was Paul Tillich's three volumes. "The term grace qualifies all relations between God
and man in such a way that they are freely inaugurated by
God and in no way dependent on anything the creature
does or desires."[1] Tillich's definition is something short of
gripping; his abstractions at best stretched one's mind. His
philosophical theology rarely touched my heart.

---

1. Paul Tillich, *Systematic Theology*, vol. I (Chicago, Illinois: University of
Chicago Press, 1967), 285.

Karl Barth, in his monumental *Church Dogmatics*, is also germanicly abstract. In volume II, on *The Doctrine of God*, he defines grace as God's "unconditional, transcendent condescension."

> "Grace is the distinctive mode of God's being in so far as it seeks and creates fellowship by its own free inclination and favor, unconditioned by any merit or claim in the beloved, but also unhindered by any unworthiness or opposition in the latter—able, on the contrary, to overcome all unworthiness and opposition."[2]

I was about to move on when I looked up the following reference that took on new meaning in light of so much that has characterized the "Toronto Blessing": "God's glory is His overflowing, self-communicating joy. By its very nature it is that which gives joy.... And where it is really recognized, it is recognized in this quality, with its peculiar power and characteristic of giving pleasure, awakening desire, and creating enjoyment."[3] One wonders what Barth would have made of the "holy laughter"!

Roughly a century earlier, the preacher-theologian, C.H. Spurgeon wrote of grace in concrete terms:

> "Faith occupies the position of a channel or conduit pipe. Grace is the fountain and the stream.... Our life is found in 'looking to Jesus' (Hebrews 12:2), not in looking to our own faith. By faith all things become possible to us. Yet, the power is not in the faith but in God in whom faith relies.... See, then, that the weakness of your faith will not destroy you. A trembling hand may receive a golden gift.... The power lies in the grace of God, and not in our faith.... Think more of Him to whom you look than of the look itself. You must look away even from your own

2. Karl Barth, *Church Dogmatics*, vol. II. (Edinburgh: T.T. Clarke, 1957), 353.
3. *Ibid.*, 653.

looking and see nothing but Jesus and the grace of God revealed in Him."[4]

Three hundred years earlier still, the pastor-theologian, John Calvin, reflected on Psalm 59:10, "My God, in His unfailing love, will go before me..." and Psalm 23:6 "[His mercy] will follow me...." In his comments, Calvin quoted Augustine: "Grace anticipates unwilling man that he may will; it follows him willing that he may not will in vain." Calvin closed with Bernard of Clairvaux's prayer: "Draw me, however unwilling, to make me willing; draw me, slow-footed, to make me run."[5]

Forty years earlier, Martin Luther wrote of grace in his *Preface to the Acts of the Apostles*: "It should be noted that by this book St. Luke teaches...that the true and chief article of Christian doctrine is this: we must be justified alone by faith in Jesus Christ, without any contribution from the law or help from our works.... It all adds up to one thing: we must come into grace."[6]

The Baptism From Above

The following is a study of the Acts of the Apostles and its two controlling themes. The first of these is the outpouring of the Spirit on the first disciples; the second is the spread of Christian faith through the conversion and baptism of new believers. A close study of these twin dynamics is especially germane in this current outpouring as it brings revival and empowers for evangelism, for the controlling message throughout the Book of Acts is *all is grace*.

---

4. C.H. Spurgeon, *All of Grace* (Springdale, Pennsylvania: Whitaker House, 1981), 45.
5. John Calvin, *Institutes of the Christian Religion*, II.3.12, trans. F.L. Battles. (Philadelphia, Pennsylvania: Westminster Press, 1960), 306.
6. Martin Luther, "Word and Sacrament," *Luther's Works*, vol. 35 (St. Louis, Missouri: Concordia Publishing House, 1963), 363.

Though "The Acts of the Apostles" is the name of the book, its author, Luke, makes it clear at the outset that it is the companion volume to his written Gospel, and as such, it is the continuing record of what is now the second period, or phase, of Jesus' work. Because the Gospel of John is sandwiched in between the two volumes of Luke's work, we may miss just how closely the Acts of the Apostles flows directly from Luke's account of the Gospel of Jesus Christ. The opening verse of Acts makes this connection abundantly clear: "In the first part of my work, Theophilus (literally 'God-lover'), I gave an account of all that Jesus did and taught from the beginning until the day when he was taken up to heaven...."

In Acts, what Jesus commenced in the flesh as recorded in the Gospel, He now continues in His new humanity, the Church, through the leadership of the apostles. Luke makes it clear that there is a pivotal moment in this transition: his account of the gospel ends with the resurrection and ascension, thereby bringing to an end the story of Jesus. The Acts of the Apostles marks a new beginning, commencing with a retelling of the Lord's ascension. But this time it is connected, not with what has gone before, namely the resurrection, but with what follows, Pentecost. In other words, the ascension "finishes" the story of Jesus, and at the same time, marks the "beginning" of the story of His Church.

In a sermon titled, "The Spirit Giveth Life," the Danish theologian, Soren Kierkegaard preached on these opening verses from Acts:

> "There sit twelve men, all of them belonging to that class of society which we call the common people. They had seen Him whom they adored as God, their Lord and Master, crucified; as never before could it be said of anyone even in the remotest, it can be said of them that they had seen everything lost. It is true, He thereupon went triumphantly to heaven—but in this way also He is lost to them: and now they sit and wait for the Spirit to be imparted to them, so that thus...these twelve men are to

transform the world—and that on the most terrible terms, against its will. Truly, here the understanding is brought to a standstill!"[7]

If our understanding has not been "brought to a standstill" in this fresh move of the Spirit, let us at least proceed slowly as we reconsider familiar texts. In Acts 1:4 and 8, Luke provides a summary of the last encounter the disciples had with the resurrected Jesus: "While He was in their company He directed them not to leave Jerusalem. 'You must wait,' He said, 'for the gift promised by the Father, of which I told you. ... But you will receive power when the Holy Spirit comes upon you; and you will bear witness for Me in Jerusalem, and throughout all Judea and Samaria, and even in the farthest corners of the earth.' "

Before we proceed, it serves to note Luke's purpose for his account of the Gospel. He is giving an account of "all that Jesus did and taught from the beginning until the day when He was taken up to heaven, after giving instructions to the apostles whom He had chosen." We so quickly skim over these introductory lines that serve as summary. Few readers will have noted, for instance, that the rendering of Acts 1:2 is missing a phrase that is key to Luke's understanding, not only of the ministry of Jesus, but of the ministry of the disciples as they live as the Lord's witnesses. The instruction that Jesus gave to His disciples was "*through* the Holy Spirit." Luke here indicates how Jesus conducted His ministry. He does so, not on His own, but as the gospel makes it clear, "armed with the power of the Holy Spirit."[8]

After His ascension, Jesus is no longer physically, bodily present to His followers. But through them, He continues His ministry through the Holy Spirit. To make this essential

7. Soren Kierkegaard, *For Self-Examination*, trans. Walter Lowrie. (Princeton, New Jersey: Princeton University Press, 1941), 105.
8. Luke 4:14.

dynamic crystal clear, Luke will not have the Spirit's work in the Church understood to be separate, independent, or dissociated from Jesus. In terms of the giving and receiving of the Spirit, and the evangelism and mission that is the fruit of the impartation, we must closely examine the key texts in Acts.

Acts 1:4-5

These opening directives are foremost to our considerations: "...He directed them not to leave Jerusalem. 'You must wait,' He said, 'for the gift promised by the Father...within the next few days you will be baptized with the Holy Spirit.' " This text makes it clear that in terms of the coming of the Spirit, there are absolutely no conditions imposed.

The first disciples were told, not that they had to remain in Jerusalem; but that they were not to depart, they were not to move away, they were not to get scattered. Secondly, they were to wait, but that is not where the emphasis lies in the text. Rather, this instruction is more pastoral than it is spatial. The instruction to "remain" and to "wait" is more of an admonition against discouragement: "It's not over yet!" There is a sense of an anticipatory directive. Something "big" was about to happen, and it was the Lord's intention that none of them miss out.

It was nothing to which they had to apply themselves, however, for the focus of these verses makes it clear that the Holy Spirit is given as a gift. The baptism is not "the opportunity," "responsibility," "quest," or even "privilege" of the believer, but "the promise of the Father."[9] Here an implicit contrast has been struck, for in Judaism knowing the "promise" was dependant on the keeping of the Law. But this gave rise to what has been noted as "the uncertainty of Judaism." The rabbis reflected on this tension:

> " 'God keeps to what He says, but am I among those who will inherit the promises if I do not keep the Law?' 'David

---

9. Acts 1:4.

said: Lord of the world, I may confidently hold fast to Thee...that Thou wilt reward the righteous in the future; but I do not know whether my portion will be among them or not.' "[10]

There is no "but" in Acts 1:4, for there are no conditions that must be met before the gift is given. This is a fundamental gospel essential that cannot be overstated, especially when in some revival circles there is counsel to "press in" and "take hold" of the blessing of God. Some even cite that obscure text in Matthew 11:12, that "the kingdom of Heaven has been subjected to violence and violent men are taking it by force." Desperate believers are encouraged in a militant, forceful seizing of the appointed hour. But all of that is our works, not God's grace. It misses the gospel by a covenant, for in the Rabbinic tradition it was clearly taught that there was an inseparable link between the Holy Spirit and a life which is obedient to God. Outside of Christ,

> "the gift of the Spirit is especially viewed as a reward for a righteous life. Possession of the Spirit is in the first instance the result of a righteous life, not the basis of such a life.... Rabbi Nehemiah concludes: 'He who undertakes a commandment in faith, is worthy that the Holy Spirit rests upon him.' Rabbi Acha says, 'He who studies [Torah] with the intention of doing it, *deserves* the gift of the Holy Spirit.' 'He who sacrifices himself for Israel will receive the wages of honour, greatness, and the Holy Spirit.' "[11]

The Apostle Paul meets this dynamic head-on, contrasting Law and promise, human effort and God's free gift of

---

10. *Theological Dictionary of the New Testament*, vol. II, G. Kittel, ed. (Grand Rapids, Michigan: William B. Eerdmans Pub. Co.), 580.
11. *Ibid.*, vol. VI, 383. Emphasis added.

grace. It is the very point of his central theological argument in Romans 4:13-16:

> It was not through law that Abraham and his descendants were given the promise…. If the heirs are those who hold by the law, then faith becomes pointless and the promise goes for nothing. … The promise was made on the ground of faith in order that it might be a matter of sheer grace….

The Law and grace are polar opposites; the promise is no longer promise if it has anything to do with the Law. If the promise is something to be attained or earned, it is no longer gift. "If the inheritance is by legal right, then it is not by promise; but it *was* by promise that God bestowed it as a free gift on Abraham."[12]

The Ground on Which We Stand

The four major Spirit passages in the Book of Acts are foundational texts from which we understand and live out the grace of our life in Christ, regardless of our subjective experiences or physical manifestations of His Spirit's presence and power.

One of the greatest pastoral challenges in the midst of this gracious outpouring is raised by those who feel they've "missed out," that they "haven't received anything," that they've been "passed by." A close study of Acts 1:4-8, the pre-Pentecost announcements; Acts 2:1-39, the account of Pentecost and Peter's first sermon; Acts 8:4-20, the conversion, baptism, and subsequent impartation of the Spirit in Samaria; and Acts chapter 10, especially verses 45 and 46 and 11:17, the conversion and Spirit baptism of the Caesarean Cornelius and his household serve well in laying foundational groundwork for all that God is doing in this season.

---

12. Galatians 3:18.

In each passage there is an essential modifier that qualifies or characterizes what is taking place. The reference is either to *epaggelian tou pneumatos tou hagiou*, or *dorean tou hagiou pneumatos*, the "promise of the Holy Spirit" or the "gift of the Holy Spirit," received from God, through faith in Jesus Christ. Either modifier makes it clear that the Spirit is never achieved or obtained through any human effort.

Even the time frame that is named in Acts 1:5 declares grace: the promise will come "within the next few days," "soon," without any connection to the disciples' readiness or preparedness. Further study of the phrase, "you will be baptized," makes this point even more emphatically. The grammatical voice of the promised baptism is passive (*baptisthesesthe*). The passive voice means that one is acted upon. If an active verb form were to have been used, the meaning would imply the subject's action: "baptize yourselves," or, "get baptized." The passive means just the opposite: the baptism of the Spirit is not the result of the disciples' initiative, but of the Father's purposed will. This passivity on the part of the apostles is similarly declared in the final word in chapter 2, verse 2: "where they were sitting." They were not required to be praying, or fasting, or yielding, or tithing—just sitting. Luke is carefully relaying the fact that no activity on anyone's part can diminish the coming of the Spirit as an unearned gift.

This is mirrored in the final promise of the resurrected Jesus in Luke's Gospel: "Wait here until you are clothed [*endusesthe*] with power from on high."[13] The verb tense and mood here is aorist subjunctive—the sense is that of submitting as another helps you into your jacket. Again, receiving "the gift promised" is not a human or even spiritual achievement, for the text makes it clear that the gift's source is "from on high," "from heaven,"[14] above and beyond anyone's

---

13. Luke 24:49.
14. Luke 2:2.

reach or grasp. The only one "making things happen" is the Father.

Grammatically, it would have been possible to have used the subjunctive voice for the promise in Acts 1:5. The subjunctive literally means to join or add to something. The subjunctive verb form is used to express condition, contingency, possibility. It would then be rendered as "You *may*, you *might*, you *can be* baptized with the Holy Spirit." But such a declaration would send some into a never-ending spiral of soul-searching introspection—"Am I worthy? Do I deserve such a gift? Do I have enough faith?" Alternatively, the imperative could have been used. It would then take on the sense of something commanded, "You *must* be baptized." And then, there would be work for us to do. The linear thinkers among us would soon generate "five essential steps" that unfailingly guarantee the baptism.

The good news is that the promise is simple future indicative. The indicative is used to assert fact: "You *will be* baptized." There are absolutely no demands made or conditions named; there is nothing to be added in terms of human effort, nor is there any suggested uncertainty as to the promise's fulfillment.

Notice too that Jesus did not promise the Spirit only to "some," to those who were spiritually prepared, those who were humble enough, hungry enough, broken, or those who were empty enough to be filled. Although the spiritual dispositions of humility, hunger, brokenness, and emptiness serve us well, they are not prerequisites for receiving the gift of the Holy Spirit. The promise of the Father is given to every believer present, without exception or qualification, every time, from the 120 at Pentecost to the 12 believers at Ephesus. Nowhere in Acts does a select group of believers receive the Holy Spirit while others are excluded or "passed over." Concluding his comments on these opening verses in Acts, Bruner puts the heart of the proclamation succinctly: "The Holy Spirit comes as inclusively as He does unconditionally. Both belong to His character as gift."[15]

Acts 1:6-8

End-time theology holds a certain unbalanced attraction for some. In Acts 1:6-8, Jesus refocuses the apostles' curiosity and speculations about the coming of the future Kingdom and puts it squarely on *mission and evangelism*. That, and not eschatology, will characterize their ministry. Further, it is made clear that this is not something that the disciples do on their own, at their own initiative, in their own strength. In Acts 1:8 the phrase, "you will receive power," is again in the simple future tense rather than the subjunctive or imperative. It is a sovereign declaration, and neither a possibility nor a command. Further, perhaps even the preposition used as the Holy Spirit comes "upon" them is declarative of the sovereign, gracious givenness of the Spirit. He does not come from "within" them; the empowerment they need is not to be called forth from emotional or even spiritual longings or disciplines on their part.

This sovereign impartation of power has express purpose, for Jesus declares, "you shall be My witnesses." The following testimonies show how the Lord used two people in this very way.

In July 1995, Vineyard pastor Steve Phillips was preaching at the renewal services hosted at the Tabernacle Church in Melbourne, Florida. His theme was prophetic evangelism. Tami describes the consequences this teaching had on her.

"I was privileged one night to be in a renewal service where Steve Phillips was sharing. I was so stirred as I listened to him share about how it's like our heavenly Father has a family business and allows us as His children the privilege of working alongside Him. He also shared that when

---

15. Frederick Dale Bruner, *A Theology of the Holy Spirit* (London: Hodder and Stoughton, 1970), 159.

Jesus was on earth He only did what He heard the Father saying, and that's how we should be living our Christian lives.

"That night as I left the Tabernacle, I realized that my car needed gas. It was late at night and I wasn't happy about stopping for gas, but I felt the Lord telling me to stop at a place called 'Smiley's.' As I pulled in, I noticed a large group of teens hanging out by the pay phones. The situation concerned me because there seemed to be only one girl in the midst of several boys. As I stood pumping my gas, I prayed for them.

"When I was done, I walked into the store to pay my bill. The boy working behind the counter looked to be in his early 20's. I must have had a look of concern on my face, because he asked, 'What's wrong?' I told him I had something on my mind, that I was concerned about the situation outside. He said, 'Oh, you don't have to be afraid of them.' I told him I wasn't afraid, only concerned.

"I went over to the side of the store to buy myself a drink. It was then that I felt the Lord telling me to ask this boy if he went to church anywhere. As I approached the counter I said to him, 'You're probably going to think I'm strange for asking this, but do you go to church anywhere?' To my surprise he said yes and that he used to go to the Tabernacle Church. I couldn't believe it. I told him I had just come from there. He said he had gone there a long time ago and that he had been a part of the 'Overcomer's Ministry.'

"He then proceeded to talk about Bob Warner who was and still is head of this ministry. The young man seemed to be fond of Bob. I then felt the Lord saying that I should ask if I could pray with him. I did, and he said yes, and extended his hand to me. I told him I knew he was at work and if anyone came in I would understand that he would need to wait on them. He told me that his name was Joe. We prayed for perhaps a minute, and then a customer walked in. I know that it must have looked pretty funny to that man as he entered the store and saw the two of us holding hands! The Lord does have a sense of humor!

"I said good-bye to Joe and assured him that this was God at work, not me; that I didn't normally go around to gas stations at 11:30 at night asking people where they go to church so I could pray for them. I told him that God had some family business to take care of that night, and that He was giving me the awesome opportunity to be a part of it. As I got in my car to leave, I noticed that the car in front of me had stalled. There were four large young men in the car, and I asked the Lord if He wanted me to ask them if they needed help. He said no, and I sensed then that it would have somehow been dangerous for me. I remembered Steve Phillips' words that we were only to do what we hear the Father saying. And then I realized that we're not meant to minister to everyone, but only those the Lord is calling us to."

* * *

Another Tabernacle member, Bob Deacon, takes over the story. Bob is a well-ordered engineer whose ministry has previously been that of teaching. He has served both as an elder and in other leadership capacities. He has been profoundly reconstructed in this season of renewal, and on this particular night, he was called to give away what he had so freely received.

"After receiving a very pointed and accurate word from the Lord through a lady who barely knew me, I decided on the way home from the Tabernacle to try some of the stuff that Steve Phillips had been talking about.

"I stopped for gas at midnight and asked, 'Lord, how are You at work here?' The store attendant was the only one around, and I got a very strong impression that he would be someone Bob Warner would have ministered to. I went into the store after pumping my gas and found myself saying to the young man behind the counter, 'Bob Warner says "Hi." ' I was amazed at myself for saying such a statement; the guy behind the counter was more amazed. After a long pause, he asked, 'You mean, Bob Warner of the Tab?' I nodded. Another long pause, and then, 'How does he know I'm here?'

"I was wondering the same thing myself! I started asking a few questions, when the young man interrupted and said that someone else had been in the store a half hour earlier and was talking about the Tab, saying that he needed to go back there. He had a look of astonishment on his face.

"He then figured that I must have a mobile phone and must have talked with Tami after she left the gas station. He had so convinced himself that she and I must have talked, that he went out to check my car for a phone. When he saw that I didn't have one, he settled into the fact that much more was going on than he was comfortable realizing. He asked me what time the 'Masses' were at the Tab. I told him, and shared with him something of the grace of God.

"It was certainly evident that the Father was working on that guy, that night. I'll never forget the blessing I received as I played my part as the Lord's witness. It was easy!"

Acts 2:1-4

The "ease" of a life of grace is mirrored in the timing of the outpouring of the Spirit, when "the day of Pentecost had come."[16] Rather than the fulfilling of conditions or spiritual requirements, the outpouring of the Spirit is dependent only on the sovereign timing of God. Again, the Spirit's "source" is named: "from heaven...." He comes "suddenly." There is nothing of the apostles' readiness, preparedness, or worthiness that plays any part in their reception of the Spirit.

This is the case when the gift of tongues is given. *Each* of the gathered receives the gift, and *all* are filled with the Holy Spirit. In fact, when all of the Spirit passages in Acts are reviewed, nowhere is there a record of one or several

---

16. Acts 2:1.

persons being passed over with the full gift of the Spirit because they are somehow unworthy or unprepared.

Acts 2:14-36

The heart of Pentecost is not found primarily in the inner, deeper spiritual experience of the first disciples, nor even in the outpouring of the Spirit, but in the ability, freedom, and authority to preach Jesus Christ. This causes a shift in most of our thinking, for typically when we think "Pentecost," we think "Spirit." But the very purpose for the gift of "other tongues" is the ability to tell other "people groups" about the great things that God has done in His Son Jesus. Here in Acts 2, tongues are given, as it were, in order that the cursedness of Genesis 11 might be reversed. The confusion that concludes the Babel story is turned so as to bring about the oneness God purposes in Christ. Commenting on this passage, Calvin states:

> "God furnishes the apostles with the diversity of tongues now, that He may bring and call home, into a blessed unity, men which wander here and there…. Wherein appeared the manifest goodness of God, because a plague and punishment of man's pride was turned into a matter of blessing."[17]

The redemptive purposes of God in Christ are clearly demonstrated in the very content of Peter's preaching, for what Peter preaches is not the Spirit, but Jesus. From Joel's prophecy, and the pouring out of the Spirit on *all* flesh, Peter's preaching crescendos with verse 21, "Everyone who calls on the name of the Lord…shall be saved." The purpose of the eschatological outpouring of the Spirit is in the universal promise of salvation, to "repent and be baptized in the name of Jesus the Messiah for the forgiveness of sins." Peter assures his first hearers that upon repentance

---

17. John Calvin, *Commentary on the Acts of the Apostles*, vol. I (Grand Rapids, Michigan: Baker Book House, 1993), 75.

and baptism, *they* will receive the gift of the Holy Spirit: "The promise is to you and to your children and to all who are far away, to everyone whom the Lord our God may call."[18] Once again *gift* and *promise* are named, as are God's sovereign initiating and choosing. Neither is the end or focus of Peter's sermon, but rather is the consequence or result of receiving forgiveness in the name of Jesus.

In our day, there are some wonderful testimonies as to how the Lord our God is yet calling those who are "far away," and bringing release as "sins are forgiven." Having been to one particular church several times, I've had the opportunity to witness the longevity and life-change of one gloriously graced conversion.

Nicky's story was simple. He grew up knowing about religious things, for his father was the choir director in an Orthodox congregation. He prayed childhood prayers for help and blessing, and as a child, he was quite sure that "it" was true. At about the same time he became an altar boy, he also got hooked on street drugs. By ninth grade, he was a frequent user of acid, cocaine, speed, and mescaline. Alone in the sanctuary, he robbed the congregational offering boxes, finding them to be a ready source of funds for his drug addictions.

Fifteen years of drug-related drama went by, until July 1995, when in desperation, he called his cousin, Mark. After a great deal of confusion, it slowly became clear that Nicky was trying to explain that his girlfriend had seven or eight distinct personalities—which were a few more than Nicky could cope with. Mark promised that he would help, but only if Nicky promised to come to "the meetings." Nicky had been through rehab before; he thought he was headed for another try at a 12-step program.

---

18. Acts 2:39.

The "meetings" that Mark had in mind, however, were the renewal meetings hosted by the Tabernacle in Melbourne, Florida. Nicky was brought to the Catch the Fire Conference in August. Lying out on the carpet the first night, the Lord graciously set Nicky free. He testifies that he was completely delivered of his addictions, not just from the drugs, but alcohol and cigarettes as well. No one prayed specifically for any of this; rather, simply praying "More, Lord." Having experienced the power of His Spirit, it was easy to explain to Nicky the power of salvation in Jesus' name.

The Spirit filled Nicky to overflowing, and as Mark tells it, "the other stuff washed out." Night after night Nicky came, finishing up on the carpet, flat on his back, "looking straight into his Father's eyes."

At the end of the conference he returned to his home. His answering machine was full of old messages from old friends. His return calls were "new messages" from a new friend with a new heart.

A year later, Nicky is still free of his addictions and growing in the Lord. His testimony has so profoundly influenced his girlfriend that in spite of her brother's recent AIDS-related death, she now knows of her heavenly Father's unfailing love.

Acts 8:4-17

Back in the Book of Acts, the disciple Philip was one of those who went about preaching itinerantly. The apostles in Jerusalem heard of his ministry: the Samaritans had "accepted the Word of God." However, there was an anomaly—though baptized into the name of Jesus, they had not received the Holy Spirit. Bible scholars have long recognized that this is a problematic situation when compared with other texts in Scripture. In Romans 8:9, for instance, Paul makes the point explicitly that if a man does not possess the Spirit of Christ, he is no Christian. Given such clear declaration, there is a glaring incongruity in the Samaritans' salvation experience.

In working towards an understanding of the situation, it is important to note here that the remedy for the absence of the Holy Spirit is not focused on the Samaritans. The problem is not with them, nor is it with Philip and an incomplete or flawed evangelistic message. No blame is attached to anyone mentioned. In fact there is no record of further instruction being required here in Samaria; Luke does not suggest that in this regard anything more needed to be learned. The remedy is simply prayer and the laying on of hands. Although we might wish that many of the details in Acts 8 were clearer, this much is certain: as it was at Pentecost, so it is subsequently—the impartation of the Spirit is a gift, unearned, undeserved, and unconditional.

The situation in Samaria, however, *is* an hermeneutical puzzle. If the absence of the Spirit was not due to any human error in the proclamation of the gospel, why did the Samaritans not receive the "gift" as others had before them? While scholars have a field day in their interpretations of this text, few fail to recognize that Samaria was the Church's first decisive step out of and beyond Judaism and the immediate area around Jerusalem. As such, it marked a most significant moment in the life of the early Church. Relations with the Samaritans stirred deep-seated religious and racial prejudices. In other words, Samaria was the first mission outpost, the first time that the gospel had moved cross-culturally, out beyond Jerusalem and her resident Jews.

The stalled gift of the Spirit in this unusual situation anticipates the truth that Peter fully realizes when the Spirit falls on Cornelius and his household in Acts 10: "I now understand how true it is that God has no favourites."[19] The

---

19. Acts 10:34.

Samaritans were *not* outside of God's favor. In terms of mission history and the expansion of the Church, one understands this passage as signalling God's intentional withholding of the gift of His Spirit until the apostles should see His presence and power manifested with their own eyes. Further, the coming of the Spirit on the Samaritans is sovereignly delayed until the apostles are themselves the instruments. The filling of the Spirit comes through the laying on of *their* hands. Then and only then do the Samaritans receive the Spirit. Now fully convinced that God's favor and blessing in Christ was breaking down racial and cultural barriers, Peter and John have no reservations in bringing the good news to "many of the Samaritan villages" on their way back to Jerusalem.

Acts 8:18-24

These verses about Simon Magus and his quest for more of the Spirit are a telling narrative about what not to do by way of seeking more of God's Spirit. With the other Samaritans, Simon believed in the gospel that Philip preached and, with them, was baptized. Enamored with the miracles that accompanied Philip's preaching, Simon followed him about constantly.[20] When Peter and John came from Jerusalem and laid hands on the Samaritans and the Spirit was imparted, Simon was so "impressed" that he offered to pay for the power, not just to receive, but to impart the Spirit as well. The sense is that he wanted to add the accompanying signs and wonders to his bag of magical tricks. He thought that the Spirit was, as it were, at the disciples' disposal.

Simon was willing to pay, *"dia chrematon,"* to give what he himself possessed. But if he could buy what he wanted, it would not be grace, for God's gift comes *dia charitios*, not *dia chrematon*—by grace, not by payment. In verses 20-22, Peter responds with a strong rebuke: "You thought God's

---

20. Acts 8:13.

gift was for sale? Your money can go with you to damnation! You have neither part nor share in this, for you are corrupt in the eyes of God. Repent of this wickedness of yours and pray the Lord to forgive you for harbouring such a thought."[21]

At first, it sounds as if Peter is overreacting. Why was Peter so vehement? How had Simon sinned against God? In speaking of Simon's request for the Spirit, Peter uses the verb *ktasthai*, "to obtain." This is the only time in all of Acts that "obtaining" is used in connection with the reception of the Spirit. Everywhere else in Acts, the gift of the Spirit is "received," *lambanei*.[22] In this light, Peter's response can be considered appropriate, for Simon had made two serious mistakes. First, he had degraded and dishonored the gospel by presuming that one must pay a price for what God makes free. Second, he thought that the Spirit was theirs to bestow, as if "it" were a commodity that they possessed.

Unqualified Grace

Seven chapters later, in Acts 15:1-29, there is "fierce dissension and controversy" raging within the early Church. What has so grievously disturbed the well-being of the Church is the way in which the gift of grace is received. There were some who were teaching that circumcision was a requisite for new believers, in accordance with Mosaic law; "Judaizers" is the name Paul gives these misguided gospel teachers.[23] Paul and Barnabas are sent up to Jerusalem and they tell the full story of the conversion of the Gentiles. Again, the debate rages: the Pharisaic believers insist that "Those Gentiles must be circumcised and told to keep the law of Moses."[24]

---

21. Acts 8:20b-22.
22. Acts 1:8; 2:33; 8:17; 10:47; 19:2.
23. Galatians 3, and 6:12-16.
24. Acts 15:5b.

This is no small issue; the very future of the gospel and the missionary enterprise of the Church is at stake. For these reasons, this "summit meeting" is well attended. When Paul and Barnabas finish speaking to the issues, Peter takes his turn and reflects on their collective experience at Pentecost. He then rehearses the substance of his first sermon. Drawing from the revelation he received through his encounter with Cornelius, he concludes his address by speaking of the Gentile conversions: "...God, who can read human hearts, showed His approval by giving the Holy Spirit to them as He did to us. He made no difference between them and us; for He purified their hearts by faith." Then comes his forceful conclusion: "Then why do you now try God's patience by laying on the shoulders of these converts a yoke which neither we nor our forefathers were able to bear? ...we are saved in the same way as they are: by the grace of the Lord Jesus."[25] Corroborating Peter's testimony, Barnabas and Paul again took the floor and describe the signs and wonders God worked among the Gentiles. James gets in the final word: "...we should impose no irksome restrictions on those...who are turning to God."[26]

We Gentiles (males especially) could easily gloss over this passionate debate over circumcision, relieved that it has little bearing on today's Church. Although conformity to Mosaic law is not on the forefront of most church conflicts, the generating dynamics often are. This text represents the seedbed of legalism. The questions it raises are: What is required for full favor and status? What is expected? What must be achieved? What is the underlying "only if"—"You will only know the fullness of God if...."

The apostles together are adamant—the grace of God is unqualified. Having to submit to circumcision implies that

25. Acts 15:8-11.
26. Acts 15:19.

faith is not sufficient before God; this one thing must be done in order to be fully pleasing to Him. But it's like the old story of the camel and the tent—let in the nose and before long, you're out in the cold, and the camel is in where it's nice and warm. If there is *anything on our part to be done,* how do we know we have done enough? This is the very uncertainty that precipitated the Protestant Reformation. Luther asserted that with supplements, "faith and the whole Christ crash to the ground...it is either Christ, or my own doing."

The religious exclusivism that the Judaizers were imposing was, and is, a tiny virus that eventually corrupts the whole. If anything is added in order to make faith and salvation complete, we have, even in the most innocent of conditions, the infection that leads to contamination. Cleansing, faith, and the Spirit Himself are all the gracious gifts of God. Peter makes the point that all that must be achieved, God has done. Salvation is all God's work and not our own. Christ Himself lives His holiness in us; the faith which we are so often admonished to "have enough of," God grants; the Holy Spirit whom so many urgently seek, is freely given. What a relief! It is not to us to make our hearts pure, to have enough faith, or to possess the Holy Spirit; rather, it is all and only grace. God gives Himself and all His gifts, unearned, and unachieved.

By way of conclusion, Peter states: "It is by the grace of the Lord Jesus that we are saved, just as they are."[27] There is a lot of theology to be had in such a little bit of grammar. The verb tense, voice, and mood of our salvation is aorist passive infinitive. That means that our salvation is complete; it is accomplished for us; and it is without end or bounds. God's grace is everything, and only where grace is everything is there good news to tell.

---

27. See Acts 15:11.

This passage we have been considering in Acts 15 deals with issues around salvation. But what of our spiritual disciplines and devotions as we live out our life in Christ? Without diminishing either in any way, they are, and must be, response, not initiative. This realization came home most markedly at a conference in Knoxville, Tennessee. During a pastors' question and answer session, we spent a great deal of time and energy discussing the role of intercessory prayer in renewal. There were some there who were insisting that it was a necessary and conditional precedent to revival—no prayer, no revival. We were dug in deeply; somehow Arminianism was again pitted against Calvinism. My friend Alan was with me; he has a most remarkable gift of intercession. In the midst of the disputations, he began to shake violently, as he often does, still.[28] He stood, sort of, and tried to speak: "Every revelation of the Father's heart is always a virgin birth." That rather cryptic declaration silenced all our wrangling and once we recognized the profundity of his statement, it opened the way to some of the most powerful, corporate ministry I've ever had the privilege to be part of. Walls of prejudice were shaken; significant reconciliations were initiated; a sweet spirit of worship and service came over all who were gathered; and bonds of love and commitment were formed that are having dynamic consequences in the greater Knoxville community.

We are indeed called to greater and greater Christlikeness. We are to "go on in God," and "walk in the Spirit," and "share the gospel." But renewal has brought grace to the forefront of my ministry assessments. I am now continuously sniffing the spiritual atmosphere, trying to discern, "Who is initiating?" "Is what is being called forth a meeting

28. See Alan's testimonies in *Catch the Fire* and *Pray With Fire*, pp. 189-197 and 167-179 respectively.

of conditions and an earning of favor, or are things as at the beginning—grace alone?"

"You Came to My Aid Even Before I Called Upon You"

In his autobiography *Confessions*, Augustine continuously names a dynamic of grace that we would do well to recover. Again and again, he speaks of prevenient grace. The word *prevenient* comes from two Latin roots: *pre*, before, and *veni*, to go. God's love and mercy always precedes, anticipates, and prepares the way for our response.

> "I call upon You, for by inspiring my soul to long for You, You prepare it to receive You.... You came to my aid even before I called upon You. In all sorts of ways, over and over again, when I was far from You, You coaxed me to listen to Your voice, to turn my back on You no more, and to call upon You for aid when, all the time, You were calling to me Yourself."[29]

Augustine gives poetic expression to what is echoed repeatedly in the conversion accounts detailed in Acts. The heart of the hearer is prepared not by any activity of his or her own, but by the electing and sovereign Lord. The Centurion Cornelius does nothing but act on the angelic direction given to him in a dream, sending for and receiving God's appointed messenger, Peter, who is likewise prepared and directed. After telling Cornelius about Jesus, Peter concludes, "Everyone who trusts in Him receives forgiveness of sins through His name."[30]

Likewise, the Pharisee Saul responds to the Lord's dramatic initiative. In Philippi, a woman named Lydia was among those listening to Paul's preaching. In terms of her conversion, Luke tells us that "the Lord opened her heart to

---

29. *Confessions*, Book XIII. 1, 311.
30. Acts 10:43b.

respond to what Paul said."[31] Later in that same chapter, the Philippian jailer comes under conviction, again because of divine intervention. He asks, "What must I do to be saved?" What must he do? Nothing, but put his trust in the Lord Jesus. Then he will be saved.[32] Some Athenians in chapter 17 and some of the Corinthians in chapter 18 hear Paul's preaching. Their conversion is simply declared: they "listened and believed."[33]

Tales of Grace

Those clipped phrases, "the Lord opened her heart to respond" and "they listened and believed," will always make me think of an evening spent in Copenhagen, Denmark. I had the privilege of preaching at renewal meetings in the city. Saturday night, after the ministry time, one of the host pastors, Johannes Fuchs, took me to the infamous red-light district. Several years earlier, as Johannes had been praying around the streets of the city, he found himself in that section of town. There the Lord spoke to him: "Johannes, it is for the sake of these people that I have called you to Copenhagen."

Four years later he received a phone call from a Pentecostal pastor who had a small café outreach to the drug addicts. Johannes had preached there a few times, but his involvement had, up to this point, been limited. The pastor said, "Our congregation has to close the café because of a lack of willing workers. We have talked about you with our elders and we have agreed that if you will take over the leadership we will give it to you and your church—the chairs, tables, coffee machines, cups, as well as the DKK 50,000 ($12,000) in the bank."

---

31. Acts 16:14b.
32. See Acts 16:26-31.
33. Acts 17:34; 18:8.

Johannes took over the work, but he and his helpers found that very few drug addicts and prostitutes came to the café. The girls could not afford to leave the streets for a coffee break. Once they realized this sad fact, the café workers went to them. In the late hours of the winter night they would go out onto the streets with thermoses of hot chocolate and coffee. They would walk up to those huddled together and ask, "Have you had a hard day? Here, warm yourself with a drink of something hot." As relationships grew, so did the off-hour visits to the café.

This street-front ministry is appropriately called the *Klippen*, Danish for the "Rock." Johannes says their mission mandate is simple: they serve coffee, bread, and Jesus.

The business management gurus maintain that there are three keys to success: location, location, location. The *Klippen* is certainly in the right place. We arrived shortly after 12:30 in the morning and parked the car a block from the café on a small side street. As we started to walk Johannes pointed and said, "Over there, a drunken sailor was murdered by a prostitute's boyfriend the previous week. They needed his money roll so they could buy their drugs." We continued our tour. On the street in front of the café was a used syringe. Next door to the street café is a brothel, red neon lights and all. Immediately across the street is a heavy-duty porn video store. On the other corners are two tattoo shops, one of which is the Hell's Angels' front for their drug dealings. There are at least four sex shops within a block radius, one of which is exclusively for homosexuals. The "Men's Home" is down the street a block, providing cheap housing and meals for destitutes. Prostitutes hang about on block after block; cars cruise by and pick up girl after girl. Twice knowingly, we passed men exchanging money for drugs.

Walking with Johannes and his wife, Ann Lis, and co-workers, Lars and Ulla, was a most remarkable experience.

After four years of consistent, loving service, the girls and the drug addicts know how much these folks love them. Johannes spoke by name to about 50 of his street friends in the space of our 20-minute tour. The majority that we met were heavily stoned. One woman kept sniffing up the cocaine dribble in her nose. So many of those to whom I was introduced had such empty eyes, and broken bodies.

One girl was strikingly different. From half a block away, a being-redeemed prostitute shouted, "Pastor!" She came running up and gave Johannes a big hug. They introduced me as their friend, and because of her trust and honor of Johannes and his coworkers, favor was extended to me. It had happened time and again on our walk, and so surprised me. I have worked briefly in a medium security prison, and I know the agony of having to earn favor. But after chatting a bit, Rosie, the woman, gave away her cigarette and asked if we would pray for her, right there on the street. Johannes looked at me and asked if I would. Rosie smiled, giving her permission.

We thanked God for this precious woman and for good friends who care so much. We thanked Jesus for being the very best of friends, for loving each of us so much, Rosie included, that He gave up His life, so that we could live. We gently prayed for the Holy Spirit to come and fill her life with the love of Christ...she got all wobbly, and we had to hold her up.

As we turned to go, Johannes told me that since coming regularly to the *Klippen* and receiving prayer on a frequent basis, Rosie is hooking less. She recently got a job where she keeps her clothes on and has moved off the streets and into an apartment.

After our street tour, we returned to the *Klippen*. Sitting in the simple surroundings, Johannes showed me a few of the transcribed testimonies of some of the converts now working with those still on the streets. Michael, for instance, was a heroin addict who was invited to go out for pizza with some of the *Klippen* workers. While Johannes said grace, Michael saw a strong, bright light, and a person who stretched out His hands towards him, saying, "Follow Me, and I will set you free." A profound peace came over Michael and his drug buzz was instantly gone. He remembers, "Jesus had met me, and I knew that I had to make a choice." Johannes was sitting beside him and Michael quietly pulled on his arm and told him to call the rehabilitation center.

This is Michael's testimony after seven months of medical treatment and prayer ministry, Bible study, and friendship with other believers: "I am a new creation! Jesus has set me free! God has put in my heart a love for the people I used to live among. I want to tell them about the way out of their drug addictions and their misery. The fire of God has cleansed my heart and given me a hunger to serve Him."

There on the bulletin board, along with "before and after" photographs, was the story of another delivered heroin addict, Per, who is also now one of the workers at the *Klippen*. He had used hashish for 18 years, and heroin, pain killers, and tranquilizers for the last 10. Per had gone through many rehabilitation programs, unsuccessfully. In 1993, he nearly died from his drug abuse.

Initially, Per came to the café only for the free coffee and bread. When the staff would start to tell him about Jesus, he would say, "Must you? Go away, leave me alone." Without apology, they would reply, "Jesus is your only hope." Over time, his heart was softened by their love. "The life and the love that the staff radiated—it was fantastic! I wanted to be like them. Soon I didn't come only for their coffee and bread, but because of their love and care." The staff at *Klippen* helped Per into a rehab program. He was amazed that this time his withdrawal from the drugs was so easy. His testimony: "I'm sure it is because they prayed for me all the time." He says, "I have never felt better in my life, and never had more peace in my mind. I thank Jesus for this!" Per is a living Psalm: "O Lord my God, I called to You for help and You healed me. O Lord, You brought me up from the grave; You spared me from going down into the pit."[34]

I will never forget how much love Johannes has for his flock, and how much they love, honor, respect, and receive him. Henry, for instance, kept following us on our walk, wanting nothing from us except to be with us. In fact, no one asked for anything but prayer.

That night, down the street from the Copenhagen bus station, I saw enfleshed what it means to be "a friend of sinners and prostitutes."

Last Look

The way to new life in Christ is only and always one's response to God's initiating grace, received experientially. In the Book of Acts, there are never any conditions imposed. But those who know their Bibles well may be saying, "Hang on a moment—what about the conversion and baptism of the Ethiopian Eunuch?"[35] In terms of evangelism, there are several extremely important dynamics at work here. The first is that the one used of the Lord is not Peter, but Philip. He, unlike Peter, is not a high-profile apostle. Although named as among the first disciples, he is one of the faceless 120 at Pentecost. Philip has only the authority and anointing of a believer in Jesus Christ. Yet it is clear that he is the one whom the Lord chose to lead this dignitary to salvation. Further, Philip does not suddenly come under conviction, and make a willed decision to do a bit of evangelism Wednesday nights. The Holy Spirit initiates and arranges

34. Psalm 30:2-3 NIV.
35. Acts 8:26-40.

the meeting with one who is divinely prepared.[36] It is also the Spirit who concludes the encounter—the Spirit "snatches Philip away."

After Philip preaches Jesus, the Ethiopian asks, "What is there to prevent me from being baptized?" Eighth century editions added the next phrase, Philip's response: "If you believe with all your heart, you may." Because it is well established as a late addition, most Bibles put this in the margins or footnotes.[37] This is not hypercritical nit-picking, but an imperative distinction: nowhere else in all of Scripture is believing with all one's heart made the condition for salvation. None of us yet believes with all our hearts. As we each pray, "Lord, I believe; help me in my unbelief," we rest in the knowledge that all is of grace.

* * *

The revelation of undeserved, unmerited, unearned grace spans the centuries, and brings redemption and transformation wherever and whenever it is declared with power and authority. The "glory of free grace" was one of the distinctives that marked the Welsh revival under Daniel Rowland, Howell Harris, and William Williams. In April 1739, one hearer summed up the preaching: "The New Covenant is all of grace, the beginning, growth, and ending; He is the Alpha and Omega; it is all of grace, so this jealous God will have all the glory of man's salvation to be ascribed to His free grace in the face of Jesus Christ."[38]

---

36. Acts 8:39.
37. New International Version, Revised Standard Version, Jerusalem Bible, Revised English Bible, etc.
38. Eifion Evans, *Daniel Rowland and the Evangelical Awakening in Wales* (Edinburgh: The Banner of Truth Trust, 1985), 130.

Chapter 5

Learning From the Master:

Grace Rediscovered

Filled with compassion, Jesus reached out His hand...
(Mark 1:41 NIV).

* * *

It is as if the scales have fallen off my eyes. This revelation of grace has reduced everything else to zero. I have ransacked my shelf of books on evangelism, and I now see things so very differently.

One of the early texts I read was Lewis Drummond's *Evangelism*, which maps out the "foundational guidelines on how to evangelize in a local church."[1] Drummond contrasts the traditional "come structures" of a local church—"Come to our Sunday morning program," with a basic reorientation of ministry mandates, such that there are "go structures" in place. Logistically, he names the process: there must be the setting of goals or aims, a surveying of the surrounding community, a surveying of the organizational life of church, and a surveying of the church leadership. But as

---

1. Lewis Drummond, *Evangelism*, (London: Marshall, Morgan and Scott, 1972).

we attempted to put all of that into practice in the local church through the mid-1980's, we found that this process consumed what seemed to be an inordinate amount of time, energy, and paper. We found that systemic and institutional ills were being uncovered, and while the uncivil war raged internally, it is now no surprise that precious few were being led from darkness to light.

Coleman's *The Master Plan of Evangelism* and Kennedy's *Evangelism Explosion* at least got us out into the community, but for most of us, what we found was that a lot of doors kept slamming in our faces, and we did not get around to much faith sharing.[2] Peterson's *Living Proof* was a good read back then, and seemed to seek middle ground for the established and more traditional church: "Efforts at evangelism are often either an unannounced assault on a stranger, or little more than being nice to someone."[3] The difficulty, however, was that my "evangelistic" friendships rarely went further than nice friendships. When I recently reviewed the book, I noticed why that might have been the case: Peterson subtitles his book, *Sharing the Gospel Naturally*. Flipping through the chapters, I was struck at how *unsuper*natural his evangelism seems. The Holy Spirit and His work are hardly mentioned at all in the book.

With grace at the forefront of this outpouring of the Spirit, we are thinking very differently about evangelism. It is not a particular approach, philosophy, or strategy for the late 1990's that we need. As Michael Green insists, "It is the Holy Spirit who initiates evangelism, motivates for it, and empowers it. The ways of carrying it out are legion.

---

2. Robert E. Coleman, *The Master Plan of Evangelism*, (New Jersey: Revell Co., 1978).

3. Jim Peterson, *Living Proof* (Colorado Springs, Colorado: Navpress, 1989), 27.

No, it is not methods we need, but a closer walk with the Spirit of God."[4]

To that end we take up a basic principle of scholarship and "go to the source." That has us asking, "How did Jesus evangelize?" I concede that the question is somewhat awkward, but recognize the truth in the famous statement of the communications genius Marshall McLuhan: "The medium *is* the message."

When even a few of the various encounters in the Gospels are surveyed, the distinctives of grace-based evangelism begin to emerge. For instance, in John 3:1-12, Jesus and Nicodemus have an extended *tête-à-tête*. Nicodemus is a member of the Jewish Council, and Jesus has a wonderful time with this theologian, tangling him up with several double-entendres. The first is His out-of-the-blue declaration, "You must be born again." Most Bibles have a little note beside this verse, for the original Greek has two meanings: *"genaethae anothen"* can be translated as either "born from above" or "born again." Before Nicodemus can get things sorted out, Jesus tells him, "You ought not to be astonished!" He then proceeds to talk about wind and Spirit, a *doubled* double-entendre, for in Greek and Hebrew, the original words *pneuma* and *ruach* mean both wind and Spirit. In English, we miss the confusion that this conversation generates. Verse 8 reads, "the *pneuma* blows where it will.... So it is with everyone who is born from *pneumatos.*"

Nicodemus is now thoroughly tangled; he asks for clarification regarding spiritual rebirth: "How is this possible?" Jesus teases him: "Is this famous teacher of Israel ignorant of such things!" One can only wonder what Scriptures Nicodemus mentally rehearsed at this challenge—Ezekiel 37

---

4. Michael Green, *Evangelism Through the Local Church: A Comprehensive Guide to All Aspects of Evangelism* (Nashville, Tennessee: Nelson Books, 1992), 319.

perhaps: "Can these bones live?" "Only You, Lord God, know that." "Prophesy to the *ruach*...." Jesus keeps him reeling: "If you disbelieve Me when I talk to you about things on earth, how are you to believe if I should talk about the things of heaven?"

In terms of their theology, no one else in all the Gospels is given such a difficult time as Nicodemus.

In the following chapter, an extended account of the conversation Jesus had with the Samaritan woman at the well is recorded.[5] By verse 14, the discussion moved from its opener regarding natural thirst to living water. In the space of five verses we read two of the quickest transitions in all of Scripture, from eternal life, to sex and promiscuity, to a rather abstract discussion about worship and liturgy. This fast change of subject meets with no objection from Jesus; rather, things are conducted with such grace that the woman heads home to her neighbors with missionary zeal: "Come and see a man who told me everything I ever did."

Four chapters later, we have an encounter with similar situational dynamics. In John 8:1-11, the woman "caught in the very act of adultery" is brought before Jesus. Where the meeting with the woman in chapter 4 was serendipitous, this one was a setup orchestrated by the Pharisees. Adultery hasn't changed at all in 2,000 years. Then, as now, it is something more than a solo engagement. If caught "in the very act," the question begs to be asked: where is this woman's lover?

Might it be that he stayed around to see the outcome of things? Since it was a setup, might it be that he was ready to get in on the stoning, and so "destroy the evidence" of his own adultery? Knowing the secrets of the heart, is it possible that when Jesus looked up after sketching in the dust,

---

5. John 4:4-30.

He looked in the direction of the woman's partner and said, "That one of you who is faultless shall throw the first stone"? Might it be that *he* was the first to drop his rock to the street?

Where the conversation with the Samaritan woman ends with Jesus' self-revelation, "I am the Messiah, I who am speaking to you," this encounter in John 8 ends with words of absolution: "Has no one condemned you? Nor do I. Go and sin no more." Neither response is repeated anywhere in the Gospels.

Consider another pair of similar but contrasting encounters. In John 5:1-9, Jesus seeks out the lame man at the pool of Bethesda. This man had been crippled for 38 years. Over and against all of his excuses, Jesus has to talk him into his healing: "Do you want to get well" This man is the only one in all the Gospels to whom Jesus asks this question.

In Luke 5:17-26, there is another man who is also paralyzed. Where the lame man in John 5 was a victim to his circumstances, here he, or at least his friends, are proactive in their pursuit of healing. In the midst of Jesus' sermon, they rip the roof apart and lower him bed and all before the preacher. Talk about pressing in! Jesus asks no questions of this man; He simply declares, "Your sins are forgiven."

Similarly, in Mark 1:23-26, the demoniac in the synagogue is rebuked, silenced, and delivered. But in Luke 8:26-39, the Gerasene demoniac is asked, "What is your name?" This is the only record of Jesus asking for information from the demonic.

Another suggestive study in contrasts is found but a page apart in most of our Bibles. In Luke 19:3, we read that the tax collector, Zacchaeus "was eager to see what Jesus looked like...." I have written in the margin of my Bible, "Luke 5:27-29." There, Jesus calls another tax collector to follow. Levi leaves all for a new Master, and throws a blowout of a party to introduce Jesus to all his old friends. Conjecture: Had Zacchaeus missed Levi's "tax collector's bash" held in honor of Jesus but heard so much about Him that he wanted to find out for himself what all the fuss was? Might Levi have insisted, "Zacchaeus, if you ever get a chance to meet Jesus, do whatever you have to do to get near Him"? And might Levi have mentioned to Jesus, "Lord, if You're ever in Jericho, look out for a short guy with a big nose...his name's Zacchaeus. He's searching right now..."?

What we *do* know is that there was a most remarkable encounter. Zacchaeus gets himself out on a limb, and Jesus turns his life around: "Come down, for I must stay at your house today." Zacchaeus outdoes everyone else in the Gospels with his response: "Here and now, sir, I give half my possessions to charity; and if I have defrauded anyone, I will repay him four times over."

Across the page from the conversion story of the little man in the sycamore tree is the account found in Luke 18:18-23, the meeting of Jesus and the rich young ruler. Verse 21 sounds a most dissimilar response and conclusion. Jesus says to this man, "One thing you lack. Go, sell everything you have, and give to the poor, and you will have treasure in heaven." We read that he went away with a heavy heart. He was a man of great wealth, like Zacchaeus, but could not— correction, would not—give up his financial security for the things of eternity.

One final contrast: In Matthew 23:13-36, Jesus accosts the Pharisees and scribes for their loveless, compassionless religiosity. There is no mincing of words: "Hypocrites! Blind guides! Blind fools! You snakes and vipers brood, how can you escape being condemned to hell!" The verse immediately following this section is a full swing of the pendulum: "Jerusalem, Jerusalem...how often have I longed to gather your children, as a hen gathers her brood under her wings; but you would not let Me."[6]

* * *

Several things can be concluded from even this small sample of individual encounters recorded in the Gospels. The first is that Jesus is not into reruns. There is no formula to be used. John 3:3, *"You must be born again,"* was not printed on a laminated card and handed out from the street corner to everyone passing by. The Gospels record that Jesus spoke explicitly of the need for spiritual rebirth to only one person, a theologian.

Second, Jesus tunes in to each individual's life center, their controlling passion— or pathos—and He brings compassion, clarification, and a unique response. In this, the gospel is a 1,000-piece puzzle; its pieces—spirituality, sexuality, health, forgiveness, truth, freedom, work, money, fear, life's meaning, and its end.... Jesus discerned which particular piece was most needed to put life together, dependent not so much on a person's presenting problems, but on his or her core, heart issues.

In this, there is a timelessness in the way the Lord meets us; for regardless of what we bring forward as we come before the Lord, Jesus meets us where we are and takes us to our very depths, where His loving grace heals and restores the fractures of our hearts.

Discerning the value issues in people's lives enables us to bring a divine perspective to very nearly every discussion.

Although many have mastered (with significant results) a particular opening question or formula to direct conversations through to conversion, grace-based evangelism calls us beyond a particular methodology and instead invites us to be good listeners, both to the one we are with, and to the

---

6. Matthew 23:37.

Spirit. We find ourselves praying continuously for the gift of discernment: "What do you want to do here, Lord?" "How is Your love at work in this person's life?" "What do you want to free up, release?"

Again, each gospel encounter is situational, rather than programmatic. And Jesus is the one initiating. There are a few accounts of people forcing their way to Him, but every time, He is the one who initiates grace. Another way of seeing this is that Jesus did not take anyone for granted. The next person He met was the one on whom He had compassion.

Here, a single phrase can be pushed to the forefront. Jesus had a divine perspective of ***compassion on the next one***.[7]

In this outpouring, there has come such a precious and desperately needed softening of heart. My task orientation has yielded considerably; my self-preoccupation has turned markedly. I'm not nearly so driven. Relationally, the Spirit keeps reminding me of this phrase again and again, *"Compassion on the next one...."* And up and out of my single focus, there comes engagement and initiation: a smile, a kind word, an openness, a readiness, and a willingness to go as far as the next one is willing or ready to go relationally.

For instance, I had filled up my car with gas one morning, and as I handed the attendant my credit card, she asked, "Where's our sunshine this morning?" Rather than grump about the weather with her, I grinned, "I could say, 'Standing right in front of you!' " She certainly didn't expect that. She lit up and said, "What a great answer. I'm going to remember that!"

This sounds "soft" to some. What of eternal damnation, hellfire, judgment? What of the "urgency of the hour"? Having traced a number of encounters in the Gospels, this seems to be the *modus operandi* of Jesus; we could also take

---

7. I am indebted to Pastor Ed Piorek of Mission Viejo Vineyard for this phrase and some of the following insights.

our cue from the apostles. Peter finishes his Pentecost sermon with a salvation appeal: "Repent and be baptized... save yourself from this crooked generation." There is a phenomenal response; 3,000 are converted.

Peter does not run out, buy a tent, and hire an administrator, even though "day by day, the Lord was adding new converts to their number." In Acts 3, Peter and John are on their way to Temple. No doubt they were talking about mission strategy and infrastructure; how to incorporate, nurture, and disciple these thousands of new believers.

A beggar interrupts, "Alms for the poor?" They could have walked right by the guy and never even see him. But something was stirred within the apostles; they stopped; they "looked intently at him." Other translations read, they "looked straight at him"; they "fixed their eyes on him." What were they staring at? And why does Peter say, "Look at us"? This looking is not the usual Greek word for seeing, *eidon*, and its derivatives. This is the word used when Jesus looks at the fig tree, for instance, in Matthew 21:19; it occurs 283 times in the Gospels and the Acts of the Apostles. Here in Acts 3, the apostles were "seeing" something more than just with their natural eyesight; the word is *atenisas*. From its roots, we get the English words *tension, attend, attention*. This word is one of Luke's special vocabulary. He uses it 12 of the 14 times it occurs in the Gospels and Acts. It always has a strongly intensive meaning, as in Luke 4:20, after Jesus has read from Isaiah 61, "...All eyes in the synagogue were fixed on Him." The word is used as Stephen "gazes intently up to heaven" in Acts 7:55. In Acts 10:4, Cornelius stares at the angel that appears in his vision; in 11:6, Peter does the same in his dream. Paul fixes his eyes on Elymus the sorcerer in Acts 13:9; he looks intently at the cripple from Lystra in 14:9. Here, in Acts 3:4, Peter and John "see" the grace of God on this particular beggar, and miraculous healing results.

In verse 6 Peter says, "What I have I give." He says he had no silver or gold. What *did* he have? What do we have? Grace-based evangelism is not an issue of our net worth or our available resources and abilities. What *we* have is not what those around us need most of all. Rather, life change comes only through a free and generous revelation of grace that makes known the loving heart of God: *compassion on the next one.* Instead of an evangelistic drivenness, we are called to attend, listen, and love.

* * *

While at a conference in Pasadena, I had some time off and took the opportunity to do a bit of hiking. After asking the hotel manager about places to go, I got lost on his directions. I got reoriented with the help of a "local," and found myself at a fork in the road. I asked the Lord which way I should go and had the inclination to take the proverbial road less traveled. Seeing in the distance where I wanted to get to, I drove about trying to find an access point, and after backtracking a couple of times, it felt like at long last, I was off.

This was my chance to have a bit of Sabbath rest. It was a much needed break to enjoy the quiet of the woods while doing some super slow reading. I had brought my pocket New Testament. I read a portion of Scripture, and while walking I thought about how life was unfolding. I prayed both in English and in the Spirit, meditated on the Scriptures I was reading, and enjoyed the beauty of God's handiwork, the mountains and the woods through which I was hiking.

En route, I passed a man and a woman walking together. They caught up to me while I had stopped to read; I overtook them while they were resting. An hour later, I rounded a rock bluff and suddenly came upon them again, sitting in the sun, enjoying their lunch. We chatted; they passed me their carrots. We talked some more: "Where are you from?" "Toronto." "Here on business or pleasure?" "Both, actually. I love what I'm doing." "Must be nice! What do you do?" Rather than give the answer that I find often terminates conversations, "I'm a pastor," I eased into things by saying, "I'm a writer and a conference speaker." "Motivation or something?" "Something like that. Ever heard of the Toronto Blessing?"

The woman, Ellen, had, and animatedly relayed a few of the stories she had heard. "That's that laughing church, isn't it?" Her friend, Jim, looked at her and said, "Laughing *church*?" She and I began to explain. For 30 minutes, Ellen kept me engaged, asking all sorts of questions—how things began, how they had grown, and what was happening around the world. Jim was fascinated as I told stories of the power of God's love and the radical life transformation that has come for so many people.

I felt embarrassed that I was doing most of the talking and that the focus of the conversation was so centered on me. Several times, I tried to shift things and asked after their work and families. Ellen especially kept wanting to hear about what God was doing in people's lives in the mid-90's. We spoke at length about finding and being found by love, about life's meaning, about purpose, providence, and destiny.

Jim fell asleep in the sun; Ellen and I dosed off soon after he did. Fifteen minutes later, I excused myself and continued hiking. Since that meeting, I have thought a lot about Ellen and Jim. They were "the next ones," and I believe that our time together was compassion-filled. But I did not "close the deal" evangelistically. They believed in God, but they didn't have a personal relationship with Jesus. I did not ask them if they would like to. And it has made me wonder.

I believe that with all the decisions about where to go, and the dithering about finding where to start hiking, there was a very real sense of a divine appointment with Jim and Ellen. Certainly their engagement reflected that. I hope and trust it was a graced encounter. Jim was still asleep when I left them. Instead of whispering "Good-bye," Ellen smiled and said, "A privilege." It made me think again that evangelism is not so much a task to complete as it is an invitation to relationship. The thing is, I had not issued them the invitation. Had I shared as much of the gospel as they were prepared to hear? I'm not sure—I did not ask if the Lord purposed things to go further than they did. I recognize now that I had not "looked intently" as Peter and John did in Acts 3:4. I am left praying, "Lord, call the next person in to take Jim and Ellen the next step." In the grace of God, I trust that whatever Kingdom seed I sowed will be watered by another, and soon be brought to harvest.

More than ever before, I recognize that every person we meet is somewhere on God's 24-hour clock. The first 12 hours is our life before knowing God's grace for us in Christ; conversion is that *kairos* moment that takes place at high noon; the second 12 hours is the time allotted as we are being sanctified. Grace-based evangelism is being attentive to God's timing in a person's life. We then seek to help them to move the next 15 minutes or half an hour, such that they receive more of the revelation of God's love for them in Christ.

My friend Kim, for instance, stopped with some of his buddies at a local Pizza Hut. When they got their order he said to his server, "God bless you." She rolled her eyes, and said, "Boy, I need that." Kim said, "Rough day?" She said, "You can say that again." "Rough day?"

He asked, "What's been so hard?" "You don't want to know." "I want to know." She looked at him again, wondering, one, if he was for real, and two, if it was worth the risk.

She shared her heart; she was losing the war with a rebellious son. Kim is the youth pastor at the Toronto Airport Christian Fellowship, and after he had heard her out, he asked if he could pray for her. She asked, "Right here?" He checked out the floor behind her...and said, "Sure, here." "Father, let this dear lady know how much You love her. Let Your peace come upon her, and let her know that You love her son more than she does...."

When she opened her eyes, they were moist. She said, "That was wonderful! Thank you." He smiled, paid for his pizza, and left. Throughout the next day he prayed for her and returned with his friends to the same Pizza Hut the next evening...with a bouquet of roses. When he gave them to the waitress, she stared at it, stared at him, and then started to cry.

Kim did not have the privilege of speaking to her the noontime word. He did play a significant role in moving her clock a half hour, even 45 minutes closer, as she experienced care, prayer, and an open and generous heart, and equated it with a chance meeting with someone who named Jesus as his source.

Is this "compassion on the next one" something we have to work up? If it is, it will be "flesh giving birth to flesh."[8] One of the things we know in the midst of this outpouring is that what counts is what issues from the overflow, rather than what gets dredged up from the bottom of our hearts. We have experienced deep within our hearts the love that God has lavished upon us. We have the deep conviction that He loves the person we are with, more than we do. We have the confidence that the Spirit goes way before us, orchestrating and initiating encounters, such that there comes a meeting of heart to heart, even heart to Heart.

---

8. John 3:6.

Again, it is ours to listen, two ways. We open our ears to the one we are with, recognizing that the unsaved are not one single and undifferentiated lump that needs to get converted. The Lord is at work in ways that are unique to each individual. It is for this reason that we open our hearts to what the Spirit is revealing and calling forth within us for the other. We ask, specifically, attentively, where a person is on God's clock, and how far the Lord purposes to take them. Having said that, we recognize that this is a time of boldness and favor. We are no longer just introducers. This is a season of accelerated grace.

Up and Out

On route to Japan, I was praying for my time there. My Bible reading had me in the latter chapters of Isaiah. Mid-Pacific, I lifted up God's promise of restoration from Isaiah 60:19-22: "The sun [I thought of Japan's flag] will no longer be your light by day...the Lord will be your everlasting light...and your days of mourning will be ended. ... The few will become a thousand; the handful, a great nation. At its appointed time I the Lord shall bring this swiftly to pass." With a deep stirring that this was an appointed time, I was both encouraged and expectant. "Lord, let your glory fall on this nation."

The last evening of the conference in Yokohama, I preached with a wonderful sense of boldness and authority, and when I gave the call for salvation, 11 put up their hands and came forward to receive Christ—something my missionary hosts said the Japanese did not do. What they did not understand quite yet is that in the midst of this outpouring of the Spirit, all the rules change!

What happened next surprised me, my team colleagues, our hosts, and the gathered congregation. We were in a large rented hall on the ninth floor of the Sogo department complex, reportedly the largest collection of stores in the world. That night, I had preached from Second Kings 7, the story of the starving lepers who made their way into the deserted Aramean camp. After gorging themselves on the abandoned food and looting silver and gold, "But they said to one another, 'What we are doing is not right. This is a day of good news and we are keeping it to ourselves.' " I had spoken at length about the need to give away what we had received ourselves.

By way of response, I asked those who knew that they had to share what they had received to stand. I had showed how four desperate men were blessed beyond their wildest dreams, and knowing that what they had received, they had to share, they brought deliverance to their people.

I spoke of the text from Isaiah 60:22: "The few will become a thousand; the handful, a great nation. At its appointed time I the Lord shall bring this swiftly to pass." About 150 men and women were soon on their feet. We prayed for them; we asked for evangelistic boldness, freedom, and authority. We prayed that the Spirit would fill them and open doors that had long been shut. We prayed that the Lord would orchestrate divine appointments, and asked that the Spirit would be opening hearts to respond.

I then pointed to the doors of the hall. We sent these newly inducted evangelists out into the Sogo department stores to tell the good news. The rest of us stayed and interceded; we worshipped and had a ministry time. Within 20 minutes, many of the 150 had returned, several of them accompanied by brand new converts!

Chapter 6

The Fire of God's Love:

Testimonies

...how immense are the resources of [God's] *grace, and how great His kindness to us in Christ Jesus* (Ephesians 2:7).

* * *

The "Toronto Blessing" is but one of the ways God is currently pouring out His Spirit upon the Church. To name but a few of the other ministries that are also yielding notable evangelistic fruit, reports from Rodney Howard-Browne's "Revival Ministries International" cite 50,000 conversions from his international crusades in 1995. The Alpha course is an investigative group study aimed at those who want to know more about Christianity. It is home-based in Holy Trinity Brompton, London, and their office reports that there are 4,000 courses now running world-wide, and that a quarter of a million people have worked through the course.

The Brownsville Assembly in Pensacola, Florida, marked 20,000 conversions on their first anniversary of protracted meetings, June 9, 1996. And the men's movement, Promise Keepers, has called tens of thousands to commitment.

One of the songs that is frequently sung across these ministries is "The River of God," by Andy Park. The theme is taken from Ezekiel's vision in chapter 47: "...I saw a spring of water issuing towards the east from under the threshold of the temple...."[1] From what begins as a trickle, the river becomes an uncrossable torrent that flows out into the wastelands, reviving life, and bringing healing to the nations. A line in the song states that this river "brings refreshing, wherever it goes." We recognize that the river of the Father's grace is flowing in many, many different tributaries. The purpose of this chapter is to give an inside look to a few of the conversions that have resulted from the "Toronto Blessing."

* * *

Harley Esson, adapted from a transcript of an interview conducted September 1996.

Harley is 34 years old and is presently a salesman for a photocopier company. He loves and honors his mom and dad, and recognizes that he grew up with parents who had been abused when they were children. His mother, particularly, was unable to bond emotionally with him.

Looking for love in all the wrong places, he married young; he was divorced two years later. He has a 13-year-old son from that marriage. Through his teen years and early twenties, he lived on the wild side. By way of drugs, he's used everything but needles. He frequently abused alcohol, in part to dull the emotional pain he carried. He has been repeatedly frustrated with his employment; his jobs never seemed to work out. Spiritually, he was raised as a nominal Catholic, and he stopped going to church when he was nine. Until recently, Harley had a dim view of Christianity, and was wary of evangelicals and "born-againers." What put him off most was what he perceived as judgmentalism.

---

1. Ezekiel 47:1.

Harley's pre-conversion boss was extremely wealthy. They spent a considerable amount of time together; part of Harley was enjoying the high living, high rolling lifestyle. Another part was looking for something more.

As Harley testifies, he knows what it is to be lost; now, he knows what it is to be forgiven.

* * *

In mid-August of 1995, Harley was listening to his favorite talk show, AM 640, "Toronto Talks." The hosts, Horsman and Lederman, had visited "The Laughing Church," for it had recently been named the "Number one tourist attraction" in the magazine *Toronto Life.* The show consisted of numerous interviews conducted with people who had *lined up* to get into the Toronto Airport Vineyard. That, in itself, caught Harley's attention. He'd never heard of a church that drew crowds like that. What really caught his attention was that he could hear joy in the voices of those interviewed. Sound clips from the worship were aired, and the music sounded great. There were interviews conducted inside, and Harley thought that all the talk about the "physical manifestations" sounded extremely strange. That was the conclusion the talk-show hosts drew: "We don't understand what's going on here, but something is definitely happening." Harley agreed, "Wow, that would be something if it was true." In retrospect, Harley had thought once in a while about trying church again. He thought about the show on the Toronto Airport Vineyard for the next month. He wanted to go and see for himself, but felt he couldn't. He thought, "Jesus, if You're really there, I can't go until I clean up my life."

He talked to his mother about church, and remembers saying that the last thing he wanted to be was a "born-againer." Nevertheless, a couple of days later, he knew he "needed" to go to the Airport Vineyard. He knew his life wasn't headed in the right direction, and he was desperate for some measure of peace.

At his first meeting, he felt very nervous. Harley sat right at the back of the church, insurance in case he needed to make a quick exit. He positioned himself immediately in front of a structural support pillar, so that his backside was covered. Then he watched and waited. Either God was going to meet him, or he'd quickly conclude that this deal was a fake. He was more than ready for a scam.

Harley watched as over a thousand people from all over the world sang their hearts out. He'd never seen people lift their hands while they worshiped. Part of him thought that they were showing off; another part could feel joy in the very air.

That night, pastor John Arnott preached on God's love, the love of a perfect Father. Harley had watched some TV religion; he'd heard the "turn or burn" messages. John's message was brand new.

At the conclusion of his sermon, John gave a short salvation message, and issued the call. Harley said to himself, *If that's true, then that's what I want.* He didn't go forward in answer to John's invitation however. He didn't feel it was necessary. He was responding to what Harley called a "TV revulsion." He did, however, go to the back of the sanctuary, and take his place on one of the lines, waiting for prayer. Standing there, he was convinced that the falling down was all psychological. "God, I know that's not You, but I think You're here. I need You, and I need to know You're real. I need to know that everything they're telling me is real. Here I am."

Harley said that nothing happened. Nothing eventful, at least. He didn't fall down when someone on ministry team prayed for him. But driving home that night, he said he had the strangest feeling, like something was missing. When he parked his car in the driveway, it dawned on him—his anger was what was missing. It didn't make any sense. His driving habits had changed. When he found himself in the slow lane, he wasn't cursing. He couldn't throw his cigarette butts out the window like he always had done previously. Out loud, he asked, "What's going on here?"

Harley went to the Toronto Airport Vineyard a second night, to try to make sense of the changes he felt were taking place—that, and the feeling that he knew he needed more. He knew that God was real. Moreover, Harley had a growing sense that God loved him; Harley wanted more of that love.

He especially watched people as they worshiped. Looking at a girl on her knees brought him to tears. The third night, he prayed, "God, it's so awesome that You're real. But Lord, if only I had a mother that could have held me." Shortly after that simple prayer, an elderly couple came in late and sat down beside him. Towards the end of the worship, the woman leaned over and spontaneously hugged Harley. As she held him in her arms, she told him that she loved him in Jesus. Harley was overwhelmed that God had heard and so quickly answered his prayer.

He kept going back. He was now convinced that God was the source of the unusual manifestations. One night, Harley felt as if Jesus had asked him a question: "Why do you always come to My house depressed? Relax. I really like you. I've forgiven you; now, enjoy yourself." Later that night, Harley found himself asking, "Father, what do You want me to do?" By way of an answer, Harley heard the Lord speak to his heart: "I want you to quit smoking. It's hurting you." Harley made a deal: "Okay. You help me with the nicotine addiction, and I'll quit." From that night on, Harley has had neither a cigarette nor any alcohol.

One night, while resting on the floor after receiving prayer, he listened to a little girl who was laughing somewhere behind him. She was in hysterics for a half an hour. Harley suddenly realized that a little kid couldn't and wouldn't fake it for that long. Knowing then that this was for real, he asked for the holy laughter. But feeling unworthy, he believed the lie that only better, more mature Christians got it. Nevertheless, Harley kept coming, and coming, and coming.

He became so gloriously overwhelmed with the realization that "God is real!" and "Not only that, He does things!" that he lived in what he called "salvation shock" for several months. During this time, while nothing was happening by way of physical manifestations, God was transforming his life on a daily basis. For instance, while driving home alone in his car, the Holy Spirit revealed insights into his father's life, and why he couldn't extend to Harley the care he so longed for. "Your dad's father was a military man, and he showed no affection to your father as a child. You're just getting to know who your heavenly Father is, and your earthly dad doesn't yet know that love, so how can you expect your earthly father to give what he never received, and what your heavenly Father can only give in fullness?" In his head, Harley wondered, *Where did that come from?* What he clearly knows now is that this was the beginning of the process that enabled him to understand and forgive his father.

The more Harley went to the Toronto Airport Vineyard, the more desperate he became to feel God's love. He was trying so hard to receive. Someone on ministry team helped him be still and quit striving. He worshiped quietly for several weeks, and then, one morning at the Burloak church plant, there were a number of prophetic words given during the worship. Harley found himself weeping. Later in the service, Pastor Val Dodd said, "The Lord wants to give someone here a deep emotional healing today." Harley responded, going forward for prayer. The ministry team started praying in tongues over him, and he thought it was ridiculous. But he chose not to let it bother him. Minutes later, he found himself on his hands and knees. The person praying for him spoke out a prophetic word, "My son, I've called you out to join my priesthood." Harley's weeping turned into wailing. It felt like a vacuum cleaner was sucking out all the pain in his heart. And then, suddenly, his bawling turned into hysterics. Everyone else was at the back of the hall, having coffee; alone, Harley enjoyed wave after wave of his Father's love, engulfing him. All he could do was laugh.

That same morning, Harley had given Barry, his father, a copy of John Arnott's video tape on the Father's love. Coincidentally, Barry's three appointments for the day were cancelled. Driving home, Harley prayed, "Please Lord, let my dad be home so that I can tell him what just happened this morning."

When Harley walked through the door, the video he had left with his father was just ending. Harley couldn't contain himself: "Dad, God's real!" The Holy Spirit fell on him again; this time, Harley was jerking with what seemed like electroshock convulsions. He managed a stilted "I'm okay dad, it's God." Watching his son writhing on the kitchen floor, laughing, jerking, his father seriously considered calling the emergency services. He knew that Harley wasn't faking, and it freaked him a bit, to say the least.

Barry came to one of the services at the Toronto Airport Vineyard a week or so later to see what was going on. He was seemingly unaffected. He didn't go forward for prayer, and didn't say much about the meeting on the way home. All on his own a few nights later, Harley asked one of the ministry team, Doug, to join him in asking that the Holy Spirit move on his father. Doug agreed to "agree" with Harley's prayers. "Holy Spirit, go get my dad, and bring him here. Free him from his pain and despair."

The next day, Harley got home from work, and before he could say anything, his dad said, "I'd like to go back to the Airport church with you." Driving there, Barry talked about how, for most of the day, he'd had this strange urge to go to the service that night. Once they pulled into the parking lot, Harley told his dad what he had prayed the night before.

Barry sat through the service, and again did not respond to the altar call. This time he did go to the back for prayer with his son. There, Harley prayed, "Please send Doug to us, because he knows what's going on here." He stood with his eyes closed for some time, and when he opened them, there was Doug, standing in front of them. "Doug, this is my dad!"

Doug told Barry how much Harley loved him. He started to pray for Barry, and Barry's flesh started to quiver. Doug asked Barry if he'd like to receive Jesus, and that night, Harley's dad gave his life to the Lord.

At a service a couple of weeks later, Barry went forward in response to the altar call, and made a public commitment to the Lord. Since then, his life evidences the power of God's grace upon it. He has been freed from his over-use of alcohol, and delivered from his depression and hopelessness. Barry is now a student of God's Word, and regularly attends one of the Toronto Airport Christian Fellowship's church plants, the Burloak Fellowship. He is part of one of their small groups, and has been to several of the Promise Keepers' local rallies. He is committed to seeing his family restored in Christ, and Harley can only say, "It's awesome."

In a conversation with his mother shortly after Harley started going to the church, Harley told her that he'd given his heart to Jesus. He then asked, "Mom, I want you to come to this church so that you know that it's not a cult, and that I haven't flipped out." She came that night, and said that she felt the Lord's presence there, but she didn't go forward for prayer. The next night, she went to a service at her Catholic church, a charismatic healing Mass, and when she got home at one o'clock in the morning, immediately called Harley. She had gone forward for prayer there, and when they had laid hands on her, she'd gotten completely inebriated in the Spirit. She said that right then and there, she knew that God loved her. A while later, the priest led her and the entire congregation through the sinner's prayer, and concluded by saying, "So, you're all born again now. What do you think of that?" Harley is amazed at the change that has come over his mother. She's on fire for the Lord. She frequently has spiritual dreams and visions, and is now actively involved at her Catholic church. Harley and his mom once went months without talking to each other; now they talk daily, mostly about the Lord. Harley is so grateful that what never bonded between them in the natural, the Lord is restoring in the Spirit.

About 30 days into his new life in Christ, Harley became friends with a pastoral couple from Michigan. They had come to the Airport church for a week, and while they were there, Harley spent considerable time with them. Before leaving, they invited him to come to a small town outside Flint to share his testimony with their congregation. A few weeks later Harley drove down and started telling the church about how awesome God is. "It could only be God who could take a guy who was raised Catholic but had never been in church since grade four, reveal Jesus to him, and then have him stand in front of a Baptist congregation a month later, telling them about the heart of the Father!"

Overcome with the Spirit's power and presence, he was soon on the floor, laughing, and feeling like electricity was jolting through him. Later, a lady came up to him and asked if he was going to be travelling in the future. "I get this strong feeling that the Lord's telling you not to." Harley didn't pay much attention. "Yeah, so...."

The next morning, he was back at work. His boss told him to go home and pack a bag. "We're going to Pennsylvania in an hour," he explained. As he was packing, Harley remembered the Michigan lady's warning. Unheeding, he went back to work.

Ten years previously, Harley had been arrested for possession of narcotics. His criminal record had never been a problem at the border, because he'd never confessed it and he'd never been the subject of a spot check. This time, Harley knew it would be different, and why it was he shouldn't have been "travelling." He and his boss were called in by the customs officials, and Harley was directly asked, "Do you have a criminal record?" Harley lied. His identity and history were checked on the computer. The customs official came back red faced, yelling words like "fraud" and "fines" and "prison sentence." For the moment, they noted his infraction on the computer, and denied him entrance to the USA.

Harley said, "I was in a major repentance mode for weeks." A while later, the youth pastor from the church in Michigan called to ask if Harley could come back in a month to speak to the teens. While knowing that he couldn't legally return, he had a strong sense of God's mercy and grace on his past life. So much so, that he said yes to the invitation.

A new US immigration law was passed in 1995, essentially granting amnesty for previous drug abusers. Besides $150, what was required was a complete disclosure of one's criminal record, current fingerprints, and medical declarations. There were letters to be secured from the Royal Canadian Mounted Police, and a letter from one's employer that clearly demonstrated that there were business imperatives that necessitated cross border travel. All of that was to be forwarded to the US Department of Justice, and after a favorable hearing, a 60-day renewable entrance pass would be granted. Harley immediately began to gather the various documents that were required to make application for the amnesty, hoping that things would all be settled in time. He and his small group prayed fervently.

Harley was scheduled to leave on a Friday morning. At the Toronto Airport Vineyard on Thursday night, he again made full confession, and surrendered all of his hopes and plans: "Lord, if You don't want me to go, make my car break down. If this whole thing is a test of faith, make my car break down in Windsor, right before the border. If it's Your will that I go, blind the eyes of the customs officials."

When he got home after the meeting, one of the anticipated documents had arrived. It was the most important one from the RCMP. Holding it in his hands, he asked, "Lord, did You really do what I think You've done?" He opened what was his criminal record, with his fingerprints appended. This is what he saw, in bold, capital letters with quotation marks: "NO RECORD."

He fell to his knees and said, "Lord, there really is nothing impossible for You. You really did clean my slate, and not just spiritually." His father was standing in front of him, and right then and there, the Spirit fell on both of them. They had their own little celebration—"Just think, the Creator of the Universe, and He pours out on you in your own living room!"

When he drove across the border the next day, no questions were asked. In Michigan, he met with the youth group, and while he was speaking, a blizzard hit. After the meeting, he was to follow his hosts home, but because it was snowing so hard, he mistakenly followed the wrong car. By the time he realized his mistake, he was miles out of town, and good and lost. At a gas station, he tried to get directions to the church on the corners of Atherton and Gennesse. He was told, "They don't meet." The man at a local store didn't know where it was. Harley phoned his hosts, and as it was late, he said he'd book himself into a motel.

He couldn't find one that was open. Signs were now covered with snow, there was lots of black ice on the roads, and he was getting more and more frustrated. At last he found a motel that was open, and bunked down for the night.

The next morning, it was clear and sunny, a beautiful Sunday morning. On checking out, he realized he was right around the corner from the church. He heard in his heart the Lord say, "What a difference the light makes, eh?" He continued, "Last night was what life was like before I brought you in. You had an idea where you wanted to go, but didn't have a clue how to get there. You couldn't find your way by yourself because you were in darkness. But when I brought you into the light, it was easy to read the signs and know which way you're going."

Some time later, Harley was worshipping at home, alone, and felt the strong presence of the Spirit. He was laughing and crying, and heard Jesus saying that He was with him, and that He loved him. Then doubts started creeping into his mind. *This is the Creator of the Universe— here in my basement?* What then flashed into his mind was Deuteronomy 4:7. As a young Christian, Harley had heard of Deuteronomy, but had never read it. In his new Bible, he found the passage: "What other nation is so great as to have their gods near them the way the Lord our God is near us whenever we pray to Him."[2] And he knew that Jesus was telling him, "Yes, it really is Me right there, speaking to you, loving you." His doubts evaporated.

Harley's son, Joey, lives with his mother, north of Toronto. Joey goes to a Catholic school, and Harley wanted to bring him to the church. He was concerned what his ex-wife would think and what Joey would feel about the manifestations. Harley prayed that if it wasn't the right timing, that the Lord would stop him from extending the invitation; his heart's desire was still to tell him all about Jesus. One weekend with his son, Harley said, "Joey, what if I told you that the Holy Spirit really was real, and that He does things, and He can touch you, and you can feel His presence." Joey said, "Well, if you believe in God, you kind of have to believe in the Holy Spirit, don't you?" Harley cut to the chase, told him of his conversion, and then asked him if

2. NIV.

he wanted to go to the Airport Church with him that night. Joey said "Yes."

Harley had some parental anxieties about how distracted his 13-year-old seemed to be. Harley then felt the Lord say, "You've done your job; you've brought him here. Now leave him to Me; I'll take care of the rest." Later that night, Joey went forward to give his life to the Lord. When he got prayed for, he "rested" as many have done. Harley asked him what that felt like, expecting "Neat." What Joey answered was, "Safe." Now, six months later, Joey wants to go to the Airport Christian Fellowship any opportunity he gets, and often asks when they can go next. He often dances before the Lord during worship. Harley says that their relationship as father and son has deepened and become more intimate and loving. Joey has become more affectionate, and a few weeks ago, Joey told Harley that his *dad* had changed for the better!

In June 1996, Harley was invited back to the church in Michigan as part of a Catch the Fire conference. Lynne Patch was part of the ministry team, and accompanied him en route. They pulled into a town called Port Huron for coffee, bypassed McDonald's and a Wendy's, turned left down a small side street, and stopped in front of a pretty dingy diner. Before they went in, Harley found himself praying grace, blessing, and angelic covering over the establishment. Harley went to the men's room, and on his return, overheard Lynne asking the girl behind the counter, "Do you know Jesus?" Immediately, the girl, Sally, started to tell them how she was struggling how to know Him, how to receive Him. They told her that she could do it right now, and she asked, "Right here?" They suggested they go into the back of the store. Lynne went back with her to where they make the donuts, and Harley stayed out front, "minding the store." After Lynne led her in prayer, Sally started to cry. By the time the two of them came back out front, Sally was radiant. On the way back to the car, Harley recognized again, after the fact, how clearly he had heard from the Lord—just in the moment he thought he was only going to get a coffee.

As Harley reflects on this encounter, he sees such a contrast to the times when he's tried to share his new love for the Lord with his friends and family at home. The contrast seems so marked. It is as though they haven't been prepared to receive his testimony; the Holy Spirit hasn't prepared their hearts, and they haven't sensed Him wooing them. Harley more than sees the difference when he responds to how the Spirit precedes him, and when, in his zeal, Harley has taken the lead.

Now, Harley asks that the Lord lead him to people who are prepared to hear what the Spirit calls forth. Two months ago at his new job, Harley was sitting in a room with a partner, discussing the sales territories that had been assigned to them. His associate said, "Well, I'm just going to trust the Lord, and not worry about it." Harley asked, "You're a Christian?" His associate began to tell him that he frequents Muslim meetings, Hare Krishna meetings, Christian meetings.... Harley sensed an open door and shared his testimony with him, finishing by saying, "The reason I think God gave me this job is so that I can tell the people I work with how much He loves them."

Harley then had to go out to his car to get a city map. On the back seat, he had a New Life tract, "How to be Born Again." He picked it up, and said, "Lord, I want to give this to my associate, but if it's not Your timing, I don't want to push him away. If it is Your timing, and You're reaching out to him, and You want him to have this pamphlet, I know You'll set it up." Harley put the tract in his back pocket.

On his return, he sat down, and within four minutes, his friend asked, "Harley, tell me something: what does it mean to be born again?" "Way to go, God!" Harley mumbled under his breath. Then he leaned forward, pulled out the tract, and told the man exactly what he had prayed at his car, adding, "It's obvious that the Lord is reaching out to you, and He wants you to know that He loves you and that His Son died for you. I really suggest that you open your heart to Him."

With that, he gave him the pamphlet. Their time together was then interrupted, and Harley left knowing that a Kingdom seed had been planted in some wonderfully prepared ground.

* * *

Harley gave some thought to all that's changed in his life. Here are his concluding reflections.

"My Father has just given me the revelation that regardless of what I am, and what I do, or don't do, He's totally enthralled with me. It makes no sense. That's where so many Christians have trouble. They try to make sense of it, and they can't ever understand it. All you can do is accept it. That revelation of how much your heavenly Father really adores you, it's that that gives the release from the condemnation."

"I know who I am if He were to lift His grace off my life. I know that His love is a free gift, and that there is no possible way to cut a deal with Him. When the Holy Spirit brings the revelation of His grace to your heart, the most important thing is to receive it. The key to receiving it seems to be resisting the inclination to judge what we don't understand."

* * *

Stephan Witt, September 1996

At the time of this testimony, Steve was the pastor of the Rothesay Vineyard outside Saint John, New Brunswick. He and his family had planted the work in 1986. Steve was experiencing the dryness of ministry in the winter of 1994. After a short sabbatical, he came to Toronto in April to investigate the reports circulating about the Toronto Airport Vineyard. God blessed him and his team mightily as they were overcome by gutwrenching laughter and fresh vision for ministry. Steve's "seeker sensitive church," the Rothesay Vineyard, was radically shaken and soon became a renewal center for the region, hosting multiple conferences. As many as 1,700 from many different denominations have attended. They have renewal services now in four Maritime cities where two church plants have been birthed. Renewal has energized teams that minister regularly.

In June of 1996, the Witt family felt called by the Lord to plant a church in Cleveland, Ohio. The Metro Church South has emerged, and is working toward city renewal with other area pastors.[3]

*   *   *

"One day in late September 1995, I felt in desperate need of an undistracted prayer time. My home was off limits due to young children; the church office was too noisy because of our Christian school. I opted for a prayer walk. It wasn't as quiet as I thought it would be. Birds chirped, squirrels scurried about, and everything seemed busy.

"This particular walk took me to the parking lot of a local McDonald's, a teenage hangout in our community. On Fridays and Saturdays, as many as 250 teenagers gather there and usually there's trouble before the night's out. McDonald's management has repeatedly failed to find a workable solution.

"As I approached, I noticed a group of teens arguing with a female manager of the restaurant. I walked up and inquired if I could help. She was clearly frustrated as she explained the futility of the situation. 'There's nothing you can do,' she shrugged. 'There's nothing anyone can do.' I

3. Metro Church South of Greater Cleveland, (330) 225-9200; E-mail 105066.2505@Compuserve.com.

introduced myself and said, 'I know a way to get the teens out of your parking lot.' Doubt and cynicism looked me in the face as I continued. 'We can bring a ministry team down here and tell the kids about Jesus!' A gleam of hope filled her eyes and with a raised finger she said, '*That* might work.'

"I hurried back to the church and shared the opportunity with my associate, Bruce Lindsay. Within 24 hours we had a team ready for our first 'McMission.' At our regular Friday night renewal service, we explained the situation to the congregation, and seven men volunteered to serve. We prayed for them and sent them out.

"Our church had been experiencing 'Toronto Blessing' renewal for six months. We had witnessed the falling on the floor, the hysterical laughter, the shaking, weeping, angelic sightings, and more. It was now time to discover if this was something more than just experience; had lives been changed, and had something been imparted? That Friday night's renewal meeting was our launch pad for some bold 'confrontational evangelism.' Boldness was unquestionably one of the characteristics of the early Church after Pentecost.[4] Some of those we sent out had never faced hard-core, toe-to-toe evangelism like this, where we took the initiative.

"One hundred fifty people interceded as the McMission team went out. While we were worshiping, our renewal service was interrupted as seven teens stormed into the church lobby. They were running from a gang of kids armed with baseball bats. Just 15 minutes earlier, we had prayed that the youth of our city would be attracted to our church and find it a refuge, but we never expected such an immediate answer! Someone commented, 'We've sown a

---

4. See Acts 2:14; 4:8-13,31; 9:17-29; 13:9-10,46; 18:26; 19:8; 28:31.

team to McDonald's and reaped an outreach in our own backyard!'

"A little later, the police came by the church to deal with the problem teenagers with the baseball bats. As the officer stepped out of his car, he looked at me and said, 'You have no idea the impact you had on those teens at McDonald's.' As it happened, this particular officer had observed the McMission and was the first to bring a favorable report.

"Just then the team returned from McDonald's, and as we went inside, we swapped stories. When our team had arrived at McDonald's, they quietly filtered into the crowd, asking questions, trying to establish relationship with the teens. There was no sound system for any worship, nor tracts to be handed out—just 'renewed' men full of Holy Spirit boldness, drawing on the deposit of hours of carpet time.

"One of the team members offered to pray for one of the kids. The teenager began to shake. That was a common phenomenon in our church, but not in a McDonald's parking lot. This was a very different kind of Big Mac attack! As he kept shaking, those looking on responded, 'Cool! Do it to me, do it to me!'

"Prayer, counsel, and encouragement ensued for hours as our men helped a number of the teens with general issues of life. One young man gave his life to the Lord, and others were genuinely touched by the love of the 'McMissionaries.'

"We had several other McMissions while the weather allowed it. One week, we distributed free hot dogs in an adjacent parking lot, just to show God's love in a practical way. This ministry was only for a season; we're no longer doing McMissions because the problem with teens gathering has been resolved. Looking back on our time there, we feel that there were two key fruits harvested. First, our people were given an opportunity to let the renewal river flow out from the church and into the streets. We have a keener awareness of the needs in our city, and an expectant sense that the Lord will continue to show us creative ways to touch them. Outreach is becoming as normal to our church as breathing is to any human. As part of two recent conferences, we went out into some of the poorer sections of our city. On one outreach, some of our people went door to door distributing light bulbs to the needy. One home that was visited had only one working bulb in the entire house! There, our team was invited in after they shared the purpose of the call. In the moments that followed they were given the privilege of praying for a single mother and her young child. With tears, she received the free box of light bulbs *and* the light of God. Our team was so overwhelmed, they gave her every light bulb they had!

"They returned to this lady's house a while later; she'd asked for some information about our church. The team was deeply moved when they saw her home, once dark, now lit up with the light bulbs she'd received. What meant even more to them was that they knew it was the same in her heart!

"The second result we've seen from McMission is that our immediate community was made aware of who we are, and what we stand for. There is a far greater sense of our 'presence,' and that our doors are open to those who are looking for a safe place, a place that cares, a place where God is real. We believe that this, in part, was why we were able to draw 65 new believers and non-Christians to a recent Alpha Course that was based from our church.

"We didn't see a great flood of souls from the McMission, but we celebrated a great flood of joy as the Word went forth. We leave the unknown results to the Lord.

"The renewal has acted as fuel for the vehicle of our local church. Whatever God used us in before is now 'supercharged' as a result of soaking in His presence. Intercessors pray with fresh power, evangelists share with greater boldness, and pastors lead with greater liberty!

"The Lord tailor-made McMission for us, for a short season. In the midst of this outpouring of the Spirit, each local church must 'hear what the Spirit is saying to the church,'[5] and walk *that* out. This is not a time for 'rubber stamping' of methods and copying what's worked somewhere else. Rather, we encourage one another with our stories of how the Spirit is working ahead of us. We attend to what is being called forth in our midst, and we customize a Spirit-led plan for our local situation. McMission was a flexible, simple response such that God's river of blessing could flow...out into the streets where it is the driest! Over those few Friday nights in the McDonald's parking lot, we touched the hearts of some teens. The larger consequence is that we as a local church saw that the 'river' flows out from the 'throne' into the streets to bring healing. If we can see Christians around the world awakened to show God's love in practical ways...who knows, maybe 'billions will be served!' "

* * *

Steve Phillips, September 1996

Until recently, Steve was a Vineyard Area Overseer for 14 churches in the U.S. Midwest. This included Randy Clark's church in St. Louis, Missouri. Because of his overseer role with Randy, he was involved in the current renewal from the very start. He served at the Toronto meetings a few days after the renewal began in January 1994, and has preached there numerous times since. He now travels and teaches full time with Equipping Ministries International, a prophetic/evangelistic equipping ministry based out of the St. Louis Vineyard.

---

5. Revelation 2:29.

"In March 1996, I was part of the leadership team for the 'Catch the Fire—Moscow' meetings which brought over 850 Russian pastors and their spouses together for three days of mighty outpourings.

"One afternoon, during a workshop at the conference, I heard one of the speakers say, 'Jesus once spat in someone's eye and it was healed.' The preacher's point was that God sometimes asks us to do 'unusual' things for Him. A moment later, I felt the Holy Spirit ask me if I would be willing to spit in someone's eye! Suddenly, all of the religious veneer of that biblical scene was stripped away as I began to think about what it would be like to actually do such a thing. I thought at length about what I would feel like if I spat in someone's eye and they were not healed. How embarrassing and humiliating that would be!

"I then began to weep as I thought that obedience to God sometimes requires humility to the point of humiliation. Through the tears and with faith only the size of a mustard seed, I said, 'Yes, God, if You ask me to do that I would be willing to, even if I felt potentially humiliated. But please—let me hear Your voice clearly!'

"Fifteen minutes later, I was asked to minister on stage and, as you might guess, our hosts brought me a young girl in her twenties who had been in a coma earlier that year. We were told that she had been on the verge of death. Through the prayers of her church, God had miraculously raised her up. The only remaining legacy of her ordeal was blindness in one eye. Immediately I felt the Lord say, 'This is the one!' My heart sank. 'Oh, God, does it have to be a woman? If I have to spit in someone's eye, couldn't it at least be some rugged old man? Besides, Father, she can see everything I'm about to do out of her good eye! I thought You meant they would be completely blind or at least they wouldn't be able to see me actually spit on them!'

"All I felt in reply to my whining was Jesus' love for this precious young girl and His gentle prompting to proceed. I asked her if she would allow me to do whatever I felt God was saying to do. 'Of course,' she told the interpreter. As my tears began to flow again, I asked her to please close her good eye. (I simply could not bear to have the woman watch me spit in her face.) She looked more like an angel than a human as she stood there in simple faith, with only her blind eye open.

"At that moment, I began to think, 'Just how do you go about this sort of thing?' As I pursed my lips, ready to literally spit across open air space, I felt the Lord suggest, 'You can spit on your fingers, if you like, and wipe it into her eye.' Grateful for this partial reprieve, I proceeded to spit on my fingers and wipe it into her open eye!

"The woman who had brought the blind woman to the stage began to weep. She then fell to the floor. She was immediately followed by the interpreter. Shortly thereafter, I followed. The young woman stood motionless for a few minutes waiting before God, until she too fell to the floor. We lay there sprawled out on the floor in front of the crowd for several minutes. To me, it seemed more like several years. Eventually the young woman sat up and closed her good eye. I heard her speak one word in Russian, and then heard the interpreter gasp. 'She just said, "Light!" She can see light!'

"We were suddenly inundated by a rush of people from the audience who needed healing. Many of them came forward with severe eye problems. As we prayed for the next couple hours, numerous people reported either complete or partial healing, including one elderly lady with cataracts so bad that she was unable to read her Bible two inches in front of her face. After prayer, she was reading sheet music that we held up over six feet away. Pandemonium broke out as we watched faith increasing in hundreds of people. We stood rejoicing in the goodness of our God.

"We left Moscow to travel to other cities in outer Russia, and as we ministered, we shared this testimony. In Rostovna-Donu, near the Black Sea, a former philosophy professor from Moscow University was healed after hearing this story. When she shared her testimony, over 60 people accepted the Lord. We left the next day with a new church planted in only three days!

"I don't know what would have happened if I had been unwilling to do something as objectionable as spitting in a young girl's eye. I do know that I am so grateful that I did not miss seeing the Father heal these precious people. I sincerely hope that this testimony does not create a rash of weird behavior devoid of sincerity, humility, and maturity. The last thing we need is for everyone to start spitting in people's eyes! But I do trust that sharing this experience will encourage others to listen carefully to the leadings of the Lord with the simplicity that is willing to suffer potential humiliation for the sake of Christ, in order that more of Christ's Kingdom may be manifested in our midst, and in our day."

* * *

Norma and Richard Iredale, Edinburgh, Scotland, October 1996

Norma teaches English and Social Education in a secondary school in a small town outside Edinburgh. She also runs the Scripture Union, which provides Christian teaching for pupils on a voluntary basis. Norma's work in the school has been recognized and respected by local Christians from several churches who have prayed for the work for a number of years.

Richard has been in full-time ministry for the past six years. His special emphasis has been on renewal, evangelism, and corporate prayer for revival. He is currently on the leadership team of a new Pentecostal church in Edinburgh.

Richard and Norma met each other through renewal, and were married in May 1996.

* * *

In October 1994, Jim Paul brought a ministry team from the Toronto Airport Vineyard to Edinburgh and held a week of meetings. By the third day Norma was so overcome by the power of the Spirit that she spent most of the meeting on the floor. She also started to "jerk," a phenomenon common with those overwhelmed by God's presence. She began to wonder what would happen if the manifestations were to occur outside the church setting. She was soon to find out!

On Friday morning of that week, Norma was studying Act 3 of Romeo and Juliet with her sixth year class. As she walked over to one boy to check his work, she began shaking and jerking violently and had to sit down. The pupils thought she was having a fit! Norma assured them that everything was okay and that this was "simply" the Spirit of God touching her. That got their attention and Norma was able to explain that God was near to them and wanted to be real in their lives. She got up and walked towards another boy who happened to be the only Christian that she knew of in the class. Once again, she began to shake and was unable to get near him. She thought it must be amusing for those watching, as it appeared as if the boy had some sort of "force field" around him that she could not penetrate.

At this point God showed her something about the first boy. She asked him if he had once made a commitment to Christ when he was younger but had since turned away. The boy confirmed that this was the case. She was able to take this opportunity to explain something of the gospel and the love of God, and then answer several of the students' questions. One of the girls walked out saying it was too "freaky" for her, but by the next week she started attending the lunchtime Scripture Union meetings with a friend she had brought along. She later gave her life to Christ. Of the 15 pupils in the class, seven subsequently came to Christian meetings and six gave their lives to the Lord.

Soon after this incident other students began asking questions about God. During one Social Education class, one particular girl took the lead. Her first question was about teachers' maternity leave; the fourth was, "How can I be sure I am not going to hell?" Since the question was asked in that context, Norma felt free to answer her in front of the whole class and explained that salvation comes through faith in Christ. Several pupils remained behind to ask more questions, and one asked to be taken to church. That pupil came and gave her life to Jesus. The following week she brought a friend who did the same.

At the end of April 1995, Norma invited Richard Iredale, one of the elders of the church she was attending, to come to the school to speak. During a ministry time, Richard invited the Holy Spirit to come as he prayed for several youngsters, most of whom ended up on the floor under the power of God. This seemed to usher in an even more powerful move of the Spirit in the school. Richard and Norma began a series of "Times of Refreshing" meetings after school which carried on into the summer holidays. The numbers coming to the lunchtime Scripture Union meetings rose from about a dozen to over 20 as pupils developed a keener interest in knowing more about God.

Richard picks up the story.

"Over a period of about three months, 16 young people made commitments to Christ. Others who were already Christians were renewed in their faith and developed a greater desire to follow the Lord. The "Times of Refreshing" meetings were never large but God always poured out His Spirit when we met. It became a familiar pattern— unsaved youngsters or "lukewarm" young Christians would come into the meeting to see what was going on. We would begin with worship, move into a time of teaching from the Bible, and then open up for prayer. God's Spirit would impact the lives of those who were there, particularly the unsaved! Many would end up on the floor under the power of God, knowing that He was real. Subsequently, they would give their lives to Christ.

"I wish we could say that it was all plain sailing from then on, but that was not the case. A measure of persecution rose up against the work. This was led by local Christians opposed to the 'Toronto Blessing.' We were repeatedly accused of being a cult, and although two of the local ministers supported us, the young people and Norma came under increasing pressure. At times this was particularly vehement. Norma was 'investigated' by Scripture Union, the national body under whose auspices she had held the voluntary lunchtime meetings for 16 years. Although she and her associate Anne were totally exonerated and the 'Times of Refreshing' meetings were separate and not under the auspices of Scripture Union, it was felt that the meetings should continue outside the school to prevent any embarrassment to the school officials. The pressure on the young people became great, both from parents and peers. Several stopped coming as a result.

"The next weeks held more disappointment. Despite starting a discipleship group in a home, some of the youth began to drop away because of the increasing peer and parental pressure. For some, it seemed that commitment simply waned. We were left with a much smaller group of eight or nine whose commitment was such that they would follow the Lord, and were prepared to ride out the criticism.

"In the spring of 1996 we started a monthly outreach at the local youth community center known as the 'Hutz.' The young Christians played a major part in this. The outreach consisted of a band playing contemporary Christian music, drama, testimonies, and a short evangelistic message. A group of five young teenage girls came to the second of these. They liked the music and were interested in the dramas, testimonies, and message, but there was no response to the appeal for salvation. We decided to pray for some people. As we invited the Holy Spirit to come, a few Christians began to manifest the holy laughter and the 'jerks.' Everyone we prayed for ended up on the floor under the power of God. This immediately grabbed the attention of the unsaved teenagers. They decided they wanted to be prayed for too, but not in public. We took them into a smaller room, and explained something of the gospel and God's love for them. We then prayed for them. They were all powerfully impacted by the Spirit of God and lay prostrate for some time under His power. Following this, four of the girls went home and asked Jesus into their lives, and at the next after school meeting, they brought along another friend, who subsequently asked the Lord into her heart. Again, a very strong persecution rose against these new Christians, and one was immediately prevented from coming to further meetings. Of the five who made commitments, three are currently going on with God, coming to church and to the discipleship group.

"It was interesting to us that once again it was the dynamic power and intervention of the Holy Spirit that 'caught' these young 'fish.' Although the initial draw was the music, drama, testimonies, and message, it was when the power of God was manifested that they were really caught. Though the numbers coming to Christ and remaining in Him have not been large, they are still more than we have ever seen before. The young disciples group continues, and it is a great blessing to see their commitment to Christ. In July 1996, we took them on mission to Dublin in Southern Ireland. It was wonderful to see God use them as they shared the gospel and prayed for people, and saw some give their lives to Christ."

* * *

Michael Thompson, April 1995

Michael is presently the senior pastor of the Tabernacle, a non-denominational, charismatic fellowship on the Space Coast of Florida. He served for ten years as a denominational pastor before joining Jamie Buckingham's staff at the Tab. He was profoundly touched at the first Catch the Fire conference in Toronto and joined a trans-denominational leadership team that brought Randy Clark to Melbourne.

* * *

"Renewal dropped like a bomb in Brevard County, a small finger of land along the Atlantic coast in Central Florida, in January 1995. A year earlier, a small group of pastors had crossed denominational and racial lines to form a prayer coalition to cry out for revival in the county. Relationships of trust and credibility had been forming across all kinds of distinct theological and methodological lines to create a fertile seedbed for a sweeping move of God.

"In October 1994, during the first Catch the Fire conference hosted in Toronto, four hungry but skeptical pastors from Melbourne ventured out to check out what God was reportedly doing in 'the Blessing.' Each of us received so much more than we anticipated, and upon our return, the fire fell on each of our respective churches. Planning began immediately. Meetings in the new year were scheduled with Randy Clark from St. Louis. Expectations began to grow during Advent 1994—the sense was that January would be explosive. January 1, 1995 surprised even the most optimistic! When the fire hit Melbourne, it landed on some dry tinder—pastors—who were desperate for the reality of the Kingdom and its commensurate signs of life.

"A powerful expression of united renewal began that first evening, and continues today. For the first ten months services were held six nights a week at the Tabernacle auditorium. They were sponsored jointly by over a dozen Brevard County churches— Charismatic, Southern Baptist, United

Methodist, and Presbyterian—a partial list of the denominational spectrum represented. Pastors and worship teams
from many churches operated under the leadership of local
Vineyard pastor, Fred Grewe, and a team of pastors who
had been given the challenging responsibility of trying to
'steward' the renewal. Services continue to be held on Friday evenings, with monthly protracted meetings to fan the
flame. Renewal leaders from around the world have been to
Melbourne, both to contribute to fuel the fires of renewal,
and to see the model of pastoral unity God has forged.

"Early on in the renewal meetings it became evident that
this group of people—literally thousands who passed
through the Tabernacle on a regular basis—were not content with an experiential joy-fest without the accompanying
signs of the Kingdom. Jesus' mission to 'preach the gospel
to the poor' became a heart-cry of the renewal leadership,
and was quickly caught and readily embraced by the renewed saints in Brevard.

"The first response was called forth when a local AIDS
ministry, 'Light of the Lord,' and a ministry to the homeless, 'Resurrection Ranch,' came into financial crisis. One of
the local pastors suggested that one of the renewal offerings
should be given to these ministries. Even though the renewal itself was just getting established and still trying to get
its fiscal feet on the ground, the decision was both unani-
mous and enthusiastic. The congregation was told of the
need, and the offering received in that evening service was
the largest single offering of the first quarter in renewal—
$3,300 was given to help the homeless and hurting in the
county.

"That event served only to whet the appetite of the Melbourne renewal's leadership for what could be done together. It soon became apparent that the combined effort
of renewed and united churches could equal far more than
the sum of their individual parts. What individual bodies

struggled and so often failed to do alone, the community of revived believers could successfully do together. Touching something of the unity that Jesus prayed for in John 17, we found ourselves the heirs of 'commanded blessing' spoken of in Psalm 133:3. The renewal leadership quickly realized this dynamic principle of spiritual growth and maturity for the larger Body of Christ, as they continued to gather and work together.

"The ministry to the poor emerging from Melbourne represents some of the 'fruit' of renewed lives. It has risen 'naturally-supernaturally' from the hearts of those who have opened their hearts and received this fresh outpouring of God's Spirit. From the early days of the renewal, there has been a desire for a river of God to flow consistently and lovingly from the house of the Lord, out to the desert places. Such was the case when God began to speak to the leaders again during their first Catch the Fire conference in August 1995.

"The conference drew leaders such as Southern Baptist leaders, Peter Lord and Jack Taylor, from Florida; Guy Chevreau, from Toronto; David Ruis, from Winnipeg; and everyone was delighted at Randy Clark's return. Scheduled as a conference, registrations covered costs, and no offerings were planned. But in the middle of the week, the Lord stirred the leaders to ask the congregation for an offering for various ministries to the poor in Brevard County. Over $10,000 was given in the single offering received the second last night of the conference. From that offering, the homeless and AIDS ministries were again blessed, and an outreach to feed street people was funded. God also gave birth to 'Project Light,' an ongoing ministry to kids in the government housing projects.

"Roger Hackenburg and Marc Telesha, pastors of the Lighthouse Assembly of God, worked with a group of people from ten local Melbourne churches, and began an outreach in one of the nearby housing projects. In a ministry that combines social action and gospel preaching, volunteers stepped out of their comfort zones and into the battle zones of the county. A children's music, puppet, and game program is combined with a relevant and fast-paced presentation of the gospel. Though this ministry is aimed at the children, food, clothes, and practical social aid are made available for families at each event.

"As credibility is built by consistency, sceptical adults have joined the children who come. Both children and adults have accepted Christ; the gospel has been incarnated among the poor. The unity of the churches and their lack of competition is amazing to those who watch. They've never seen the reality of Christ's united Body so clearly and generously demonstrated.

"The ministry began in one section of town known for its violence and drug traffic. Not only has it been received, but even the police have gotten in on the act! Sidewalk Sunday school has grown to two locations—one in conjunction with a local church in the neighborhood. Crossing racial and cultural lines, the love shared has been contagious. Invitations stand at present for at least three more locations.

"Over $6,000 from renewal funds have been invested in this ministry, purchasing sound equipment, outfitting a trailer, and providing food to be given away. Most of the more than 60 regular volunteers have risen from the ranks of the 'carpet time' brigade. This united effort has arisen like a phoenix from the fires of renewal! With the passion generated by these outreaches, Hackenburg and crew sponsored an Operation Blessing outreach. Taking many middle-class suburbanites out of their familiar surroundings, the loving workers invaded one of Melbourne's toughest neighborhoods. Gospel music blared over loudspeakers as nearly 400 workers from 36 churches gave out 40,000 pounds of food to nearly 3,000 families. Because of the atmosphere of love and unity, 140 people were bold enough to receive prayer, and 40 of them accepted Christ for the first time in their lives.

"The saga continues! On Yom Kippur 1995, the Melbourne renewal invited other Evangelicals to join them for a prayer meeting at the Space Coast Stadium. Over 3,500 brave souls defied pouring rain to gather and pray for revival in the county. An offering was received and all of it went to the ministries to the poor in the county. The renewal covered over $3,500 in expenses so that the joint offering, nearly $14,000, could be given away. Two local Habitat for Humanity chapters were supported. (This is a cooperative organization that builds low cost housing.) A food kitchen, food bank, and community development agency were also blessed with financial aid.

"Out of relationships built in renewal, meetings were sponsored by a small, African-American congregation in the heart of the drug district. Area pastors took turns preaching, leading worship, and praying in services that dwarfed the expectations of all who were involved in their planning. Unity across denominational and racial lines has led to cooperation in both evangelistic and social action efforts in the community. Not only is the fire catching, but so is the vision for what happens when renewed people take their fresh life to the strongholds in society.

"It has become increasingly clear in the Melbourne renewal that if the powerful exhibition of the life of God doesn't give an even more powerful expression of the heart of God, it is a myopic move which will be short-lived. God is not merely into entertaining the troops. His desire is that the dry bones rise up as an exceeding great army to do battle for the hearts of men and the soul of the nations.

"We've seen significant demonstrations of this locally. One of the Melbourne area churches affected deeply by renewal made many concrete attempts to cross boundaries and break barriers to demonstrate the reality of the love and unity of Christ. A middle-aged white Southern Baptist pastor hired a fiery black Pentecostal as his associate pastor. The church longed for their associate to be full-time, but the money wasn't yet there to fully support him. One day in the renewal pastors' meeting, the pastor came in to share that his associate had run into a major financial need. Before he left the meeting that day, $800 was placed in his hands by caring leaders. Shortly thereafter, the renewal leadership approved an $800 per month stipend for six months to help this brother get established. The ministry of reconciliation was pragmatically underway.

"The Melbourne renewal churches were also privileged to play a part in a Russian outreach. After a challenge by Randy Clark, we raised over $5,000 to sponsor Russian church leaders as they gathered for a renewal conference in Moscow. On top of that, over $6,000 came in to support pastors who were planting churches out of renewal throughout the former Soviet Union.

"Renewal has made an impact to the south of us as well. On a routine trip to Honduras to ferret out potential development project sights, our missionary pastor, Jonathan Smoak, discovered that during seasons of renewal nothing is routine! Community development and relief was part of the growing missions strategy of the Tabernacle Church in Melbourne before renewal fires blazed hot in the county. After prophetic promptings from leadership, the search team for a 1995 summer Honduras project went away thinking that perhaps something was up.

"Upon arrival in Honduras, and giving in to gentle promptings of the Spirit, the team went to evaluate a Christian camp—Bethel—as the possible destination spot for a junior high discipleship trip. Smoak had led development projects in Honduras dozens of times, but had never been to this particular camp. He knocked on the door of the home which housed Bethel's overseers. A stately lady named Elva greeted them and began to discuss the business of the camp—in Spanish.

"When the project was proposed, there was hesitance on Elva's part; she was protective of the beautiful facility—an enigma in the drab and poverty-stricken Honduran culture. But another gentle prompting from the Spirit caused Jonathan to ask her if she'd ever heard of Jamie Buckingham, a prolific Charismatic writer and the Tabernacle's founding pastor. Immediately, Elva began to speak flawless English and reported how indebted she'd been to Jamie's writings.

"The door was swung wide open for the missions/discipleship trip! As the discussion continued, Elva suggested that the team look at the facilities, which were more than adequate for the needs of the planned trip. When they walked into the auditorium, the team nearly fainted. The building was an absolute duplicate of the Tabernacle's Melbourne auditorium. Smoak breathlessly reported to Elva, 'This is our church!' She replied, 'Yes. I was at the Tabernacle nearly a dozen years ago and fell in love with the simplicity and size of the building. We were in the development stages of Camp Bethel, so we duplicated the building we'd seen.'

It was then that the divine pieces began to come together. Elva went on to report that the camp had been built with the vision of being a renewal center for leaders in Honduras. She stated that for nearly a dozen years she had waited and prayed, watching as the camp was used for many good things, but never for leadership revival. She had heard of reports of renewal in Toronto, but their limited resources made it impossible for them to travel that far. She had heard reports from nearby Melbourne, and had been praying for someone to come from there and share the fire!

Now, Jonathan was standing on her doorstep—renewal was just around the corner.

"From those sovereignly orchestrated beginnings, the Melbourne Renewal Fellowship began to pursue ongoing relationships with leaders in the Honduran church. At the end of May 1995, the Renewal underwrote the costs to bring 25 Honduran leaders to a week of meetings in Melbourne. Subsequently, in October, a Catch the Fire conference featuring trans-denominational leaders from Melbourne was held at Bethel; a second conference was hosted in the summer of 1996.

"Twelve years ago, at Bethel's inception, revival seeds were planted. What an awesome privilege it has been to see God harvest fruit as events in Toronto, Melbourne, and Honduras catalyzed, such that 150 Honduran leaders came into such a powerful ministry of the Holy Spirit, and equally dynamic youth renewal meetings brought great joy to young people from churches across Tegucigalpa during the junior high trip, the original reason for finding Bethel."

* * *

"Since the beginnings of renewal in Melbourne, God seems to have directed much of the spiritual energy and refreshment to ministry to the poor, to the marginalized in the county, and on overseas mission fields in Honduras and Russia. Whether in the neighborhood, in the struggling church or in a foreign land, renewal in Melbourne has resulted in a passion for the Kingdom and its expression to the poor. The stories are so easy to multiply. Recently, six beach-side churches joined together to build a Habitat for Humanity house for a needy family in the area. The Baptist pastor leading the push stated emphatically, 'This happened as direct fruit of the Renewal.' A medical and teaching team is preparing for the second *Catch the Fire* conference in Honduras for 1996.

"In so many ways, Melbourne renewal seems to be a reflection of the first miracle that Jesus performed. In John 2, at the wedding feast in Cana, the party had run dry. This fact was lamented, and in response, Jesus commanded that the ceremonial pots be filled with water; when it was poured out, the water had become the finest of wine!

"Jesus heard the desperate cries of pastors and people in Melbourne for a move of His Spirit. He reached across denominational lines and filled whatever ceremonial vessels (traditions, creeds, worship styles) that were empty and desperate enough to receive. We have been filled to overflowing with the water of life. As He has poured us out, we have become an intoxicating and aromatic fragrance, a revelation of the heart and compassion of Christ, especially to the hurting!"

* * *

Nearly 500 years ago, reformation swept the Church in Europe. We are seeing a wonderful re-formation of faith and witness in our day. Ours is such a rich heritage. Martin Luther, in his famous *Preface to Romans*, gave us language to speak of all that is ours in Christ:

"Faith is a living, daring confidence in God's grace, so sure and certain that the believer would stake his life on it a thousand times. This knowledge of and confidence in God's grace makes men glad and bold and happy in dealing with God and with all creatures. And this is the work which the Holy Spirit performs in faith. Because of it, without compulsion, a person is ready and glad to do good to everyone, to serve everyone, to suffer everything, out of love and praise to God who has shown him this grace."[6]

6. Luther's Works, vol. 35, *Word and Sacrament*, (St. Louis: Concordia Pub. House, 1963), 371.

Conclusion

Soaking With Purpose

I will venture to speak only of what Christ has done through me to bring the Gentiles into His allegiance, by word and deed, by the power of signs and portents, and by the power of the Holy Spirit... (Romans 15:18-19).

* * *

Ninety years ago, the meetings at 312 Azusa Street commanded considerable press coverage. Unlike the media favor that has characterized the reports of the "Toronto Blessing," this secular newspaper article is representative of the prejudices brought against the first Pentecostals:

"There is a most disgraceful intermingling of the races. Together, they cry and make howling noises all day and into the night. They run, jump, shake all over, shout to the top of their voice, spin around in circles, fall out on the sawdust blanketed floor jerking, kicking and rolling all over it. Some of them pass out and do not move for hours as though they were dead. These people appear to be mad, mentally deranged or under a spell. They claim to be filled with the Spirit.

"They have a one-eyed, illiterate Negro as their preacher who stays on his knees much of the time with his head hidden between wooden milk crates [his pulpit]. He doesn't talk very much but at times he can be heard shouting

'Repent,' and he's supposed to be running the thing....
They repeatedly sing the same song, 'The Comforter Has
Come.' "[1]

Pastor Frank Bartleman chronicled the birth of Pente-
costalism. He described some of the dynamics of the meetings held in the "tumble-down shack" on Azusa Street:

> "The services ran almost continuously. Seeking souls
> could be found under the power almost any hour, night
> and day. The place was never closed nor empty. The peo-
> ple came to meet God. He was always there. Hence a con-
> tinuous meeting. The meeting did not depend on the
> human leader. God's presence became more and more
> wonderful. In that old building, with its low rafters and
> bare floors, God took strong men and women to pieces,
> and put them together again, for His glory. It was a tre-
> mendous overhauling process. Pride and self-assertion,
> self-importance and self-esteem, could not survive
> there."[2]

It is estimated that 13,000 leaders came to the meetings
on Azusa street. Those whom God "took to pieces" returned to their respective homes, and nearly 100 years later,
the fruit of their lives and ministries represents the greatest
evangelistic and missionary enterprise Christendom has
ever witnessed. It is estimated that there are now half a billion Pentecostal/charismatics worldwide.

In the midst of this present outpouring of God's Spirit,
thousands would concur with Bartleman's observations:
God has overhauled us; first, we have been taken to pieces,

---

1. Art Glass, *Pentecostal Heritage, Inc.*, unpublished paper, Pentecostal
   Azusa Revival Museum, 8.
2. Frank Bartleman, *How Pentecost Came to Los Angeles: As It Was in the
   Beginning*, 2nd ed. (Los Angeles, California: By the Author, 1925),
   58.

and then put together again for His glory. Pride, perform-ance, insecurity, fear, competitiveness, and issues of control are being healed and redeemed. This work is so deep and so profound that many of us struggle to give expression to the grace we have touched and the life transformations that have been called forth.

The Last of the Fathers

Chapter 1 of *Share the Fire* closed with a quotation by Bernard of Clairvaux. Bernard is an important figure in the history of the Church for many reasons; among them, that he was able to give expression to the most intimate of reve-lations received from the Lord. He was so articulate that he earned the title: "Mellifluous Doctor," "the Doctor-flowing-with-honey."

For Bernard, theology rose out of meditation and prayer, loving devotion and revelation. Heir of the rich mo-nastic tradition of John Cassian and Benedict, Bernard's un-derstanding and experience of God's love was grounded in worship, and characterized by the maxim: *Semper in ore psalmus, semper in corde Christus*, "Always a psalm on the lips, always Christ in the heart."

Bernard was not just a writer of spiritual theology though; he had tremendous influence on the political, liter-ary, and religious life of Europe, and is known as one of the great revivalists and reformers of the High Middle Ages. It is said of Bernard that "he cast fire on earth wherever he went. God worked in him, and worked such wonders that men knew it was God they had seen at work, not man. The grace of the God who had possession of this frail man burst into flame in the hearts of all who heard him speak."[3]

---

3. Thomas Merton, *The Last of the Fathers* (New York, New York: Har-court Brace Jovanovich, Pub., 1954), 27.

In 1113, at the age of 22, Bernard entered a floundering new monastery at Citeaux. His influence was such that he brought 30 friends and relatives with him, more than doubling the community's size. Four years later, he was elected to lead a new foundation in the valley of Absinthe, about halfway between Dijon in France and Geneva in Switzerland. The monks renamed the place, Clairvaux, "The Valley of Light." Less than 50 years later, at Bernard's death, the monastic order of Cistercians had so prospered that they grew exponentially, from three to 343 communities, spread throughout Europe.

A Supernatural Superabundance

Near the end of his life, Bernard wrote of his personal experience of God's transforming grace. The metaphor for which he is most famous is "the Kiss of the Bridegroom," taken from Solomon's *Song of Songs*. Let the reader mark the following: Bernard states and restates that this "Kiss" was always *unfelt*. Nevertheless, he knew that the Lord was present, for

> "as soon as He has entered into me, He has quickened my sleeping soul, has aroused and softened and goaded my heart, which was in a state of torpor and hard as stone. He has begun to pluck up and destroy, to plant and to build, to water the dry places, to illuminate the gloomy spots, to throw open those which were shut close, to inflame with warmth those [places] which were cold, and to straighten its crooked paths and make its rough places smooth, so that my soul might bless the Lord and all that is within me praise His Holy name."[4]

4. "Canticle 74.5," quoted in Dom Cuthbert Butler, *Western Mysticism—Augustine, Gregory and Bernard.* (London: Constable and Company, 1922), 147.

Bernard preached 86 sermons on the first three chapters of the *Song of Songs*. The sermon series is incomplete; he died before he could bring it to conclusion. Like Augustine before him, Bernard testifies to prevenient grace, for he knows experientially that the love, the mercy, and the kindnesses that he has received from God so freely poured out without measure, come only as gift. He titled his eighty-fourth sermon, *"The soul, seeking God, is anticipated by Him,"* and in it, he speaks of the ongoing call, and the ever-fuller revelation of grace that God purposes for us. In terms of the awakening of faith, Bernard speaks as an intimate lover and friend:

> "I do not think that when a soul has found Him, it will cease from seeking. God is sought, not by the movement of the feet, but by the desires of the heart; and when a soul has been so happy as to find Him, that sacred desire is not extinguished, but, on the contrary, is increased. Is the consummation of the joy the extinction of the desire? It is rather to it as oil poured upon a flame; for desire is, as it were, a flame. Our joy will be fulfilled; but the fulfillment will not be the ending of the desire, nor therefore of the seeking…. Every soul among you that is seeking God should know that it has been anticipated by Him, and has been sought by Him before it began to seek Him."[5]

The apostle admonished Timothy, to "do the work of an evangelist."[6] In this present season of grace, it is clearer than ever before that we are not the ones initiating. As we seek to share faith with the unsaved, we do well to remind ourselves of Bernard's counsel: "Every soul that is seeking God…has been anticipated by Him, and has been sought by Him before it began to seek Him"; especially since issues of

---

5. *Late Medieval Mysticism*, Ray Petry, ed. Library of Christian Classics, (Philadelphia, Pennsylvania: Westminster Press, 1957), 74.
6. 2 Timothy 4:5 NIV.

pride, control, insecurity, and drivenness can so easily rise up and corrupt our best intentions. Any time we attempt to accomplish any work of the Kingdom, especially evangelism, the Lord's words need to be ringing in our ears: "Apart from Me you can do nothing."[7] It is His initiative, and not ours, that draws the unsaved.

"Belch Forth of Thy Fullness"

Bernard of Clairvaux continues to serve as a helpful resource, for in a sermon written for Pentecost Sunday, he takes up the image of new wine.

Speaking of experiences so very similar to many who have found themselves "Toronto Blessed," he works things further, and marks the progress of the digestive process:

"It is [in] prayer that we drink the wine of the Spirit, which intoxicates the soul with holy love…. This wine irrigates the parched interior of the heart, facilitates the digestion of the meat of good works, and distributes the nutriment amongst the members of the soul (if you allow me the expression), confirming faith, fortifying hope, enlivening and regulating charity, and anointing all our actions with the rich unction of grace."

Changing metaphors, he continues:

"My brethren, if you be wise, you will make yourselves to be reservoirs rather than conduits. The difference between a conduit and a reservoir is this, that whereas the former discharges all its waters almost as soon as it is received, the latter waits until it is full to the brim, and only communicates what is superfluous, what it can give away without loss to itself."

As spiritual father, Bernard takes the liberty to speak correction to those who are so keen to pour out their lives:

---

7. John 15:5b NIV.

"We have in the Church today many conduits and but very few reservoirs. So great is the charity of those through whom the celestial streams of knowledge are communicated to us, that they want to give away before they have received. They are more willing to speak than to listen. They are forward to teach what they have not learned. Although unable to govern themselves, they gladly undertake to rule others. Thy charity is either non-existent, or so delicate and reed-like that it bends to every blast."

He names the internal conflict of high and noble aspirations of loving neighbor even more than self, while at the same time being so spiritually unstable that one "dissolves in consolation, faints under fear, loses its peace in sadness, is contracted by greed, distracted by ambition, disquieted by suspicion, disturbed by reproof, tormented with care, inflated with honour, consumed with envy." He calls his brothers to a posture of spiritual stability:

"My brothers, learn to belch forth of thy fullness, and do not desire to be more generous than God.... The charity which combines prudence with generosity is wont to flow in before flowing out.... Behold now how much has to be poured into us in order that we may venture to pour out, giving of our plenitude, not of our poverty."[8]

* * *

Around the world, there are those who have grown impatient, even criticizing the repeated coming forward for prayer that characterizes renewal ministry. "How much 'carpet time' does one need before one gets down to business?" With the journalist who wrote the piece quoted from the *Island Herald* in Chapter 1, there are many who are highly committed to answer our Lord's clear call to Kingdom ministry,

8. *St. Bernard's Sermons for the Seasons and Principal Festivals of the Year*, vol. II (Dublin: Browne and Nolan, 1923), 176-183.

especially when they are passionately concerned about the lostness of the lost, and the need for gospel justice and righteousness within our political and social systems. It is asked repeatedly of the "Toronto Blessing," "Where's the fruit of all of this?" With the Apostle Paul, many answer relationally: We will keep coming forward for prayer until we know the height and depth, the length and breadth of the love of Christ, and to know it, though it is beyond knowledge.[9]

In terms of ministry, many of us have recognized that we have lived and attempted to minister, as Bernard put it, as conduits rather than reservoirs. We have more than realized that our attempts to serve only as conduits of grace so quickly leave us barren and empty, with no resources but our own abilities and best intentions as hollow shells.

Our spirits are being renewed and revived as the Lord so mercifully pours out His Spirit upon us, and we are finding that as we continue to rest in His love, ever looking to His grace for a fuller and fuller filling, the reservoirs of the Spirit are full and overflowing, and not just with a superabundance, but a supernatural superabundance. Instead of flesh giving birth to flesh, Spirit is birthing spirit. And in terms of evangelism, there are so many who have such wonderful testimonies of the glorious overflow of grace from their lives. Carla Doyle is one of them.

Over the Top

Carla came to the renewal meetings in Melbourne, Florida, early in 1995. Without apology, she came in desperation, and freely received grace upon grace. She was physically ill with severe back problems (severe spinal arthritis and advanced osteoporosis), which had put her on a disability allowance for over six years. Several weeks before her

---

9. Ephesians 3:19.

first meeting, Carla had been widowed; several weeks before her husband's death, she had adopted her two pre-teen grandsons. Her daughter is a cocaine addict, and her son-in-law had committed suicide. Not surprisingly, her grandsons had been under psychiatric care and on medication for four years due to the trauma of their life circumstances.

As the Tabernacle hosted renewal meetings six nights a week, Carla estimates that she came over 120 times that first year, responding to every call for prayer ministry, "soaking herself" in the love of her Father, and allowing the Spirit to heal more and more of her heart. She committed herself completely to God, and asked Him to make her and the boys whole. She then told Him that she wanted to be His vessel in any way He chose.

Gently, yet systematically, God began to work in her life and the lives of her boys. For 30 years, Carla was chemically dependent on prescribed anti-depressants, but no longer. Both her grandsons no longer need their medications, nor the psychiatric care. The pain and physical immobility of Carla's back problems have nearly disappeared.

In March of 1996, this 56-year-old grandmother and her eight and nine-year-old boys left for five months of training and field duty with Mercy Ships International. After three months of schooling, they spent two months in Puerto Cabezas, Nicaragua, where Carla was asked to coordinate local evangelism. She served five different church denominations, several schools, an orphanage, a prison, as well as a street ministry. She and her team did everything from well drilling to teaching personal hygiene; they refurbished a children's playground and prayed for dying children. They had the privilege of seeing people come to the Lord through their personal witnessing.

At the conclusion of her field training, Carla returned home. She is furthering her studies and is worshiping with her home church. These are her concluding remarks:

"I have returned to renewal here at the Tabernacle in anticipation of what God will show me through this ministry. I pray for more of God's anointing and the opportunity to minister to others with what He's already given me. But most of all, I pray to once again exalt Him on the mission field."

* * *

Learning to See

Obviously, not all of us are called to the nations. But this present outpouring of God's Spirit *is* preparing His Church for the end-time harvest, whenever the Lord sovereignly calls it in. That *is* the eschatological horizon toward which we are moving.

Wherever the Lord has us, with whomever the Lord has us, the salvation of the lost is His heart's desire. It is ours to have compassion on the next one. Here, we have a wonderful freedom, for we know that God's lovingkindness goes before us. As we meet with friends and strangers, we call forth one of the distinctives of grace-based evangelism—discernment.

It is as if we each have a window to our spirits. And it is only spiritual discernment that enables us to perceive how wide open the window of faith is in a particular individual. If it is closed, it does not serve to smash it in, or to try to pry it open. Again and again in the Gospels, most of the Pharisees were closed, locked, and barred; Nicodemus was an exception. Further, the rich young ruler walked away *from Jesus*. His window was boarded over by materialism.

There were times, however, when the pendulum was swung to the other extreme. The centurion from Capernaum threw his window wide open: "...But say the word...."

Jesus remarks: "Not even in Israel have I found such faith."[10]

Evangelism is by its very nature a supernatural work. As we have compassion on the next one, we are also asking continuously, "How are You at work here Father? What have You orchestrated for this encounter, this moment?" As we seek to discern what it is the Lord has purposed, we recognize that it is not so much the case that we have to "do or say something." Rather, we *search our hearts*. We search our hearts for the love that our heavenly Father has for the person we are with. Here the heart leads, and the mind serves. Is there love reaching out, and love being revealed? Or is our motive for involvement driven by performance? Are we seeking to impress someone? Is it an issue of spiritual ego or superiority? Or, do we quickly and continuously remember our grounding in grace, and pray for a further measure of compassion and mercy?

Spiritual gifts and grace flow through love inspired by the Spirit, not through technique and methodology. In the Gospels, we read repeatedly that "His heart went out to them." "He had compassion on them...."[11]

* * *

Radical Abandon

This much is safe. The dynamics at work in the "Toronto Blessing" have stretched most of us, such that we recognize that far more is at work in this day. Many were taken far beyond their proverbial comfort zones during the second anniversary week at the Toronto Airport Christian Fellowship, for which over 3,000 believers had gathered. One evening,

10. Luke 7:7-9.
11. Matthew 9:36; 14:14; 15:32; 20:34; Mark 1:41; 6:34; 8:2; Luke 7:13; cf. Luke 15:20, the prodigal's father.

Paul Cain was preaching. Paul can be considered one of our generation's prophetic grandfathers. He is a senior states-man for the Body of Christ; it was a high privilege to have him take part in our anniversary celebrations.

His message that particular night was titled, "Dignity or the Anointing." Early into the sermon, a gentleman in the second row started "Oh-ing." He got louder and louder. John Arnott looked in his direction, smiled, and told the surrounding ministry team to soak him. As they prayed, he manifested more and more boisterously. He was soon on the floor; not long thereafter, he had crawled underneath the front row of chairs, and was in the open ministry area, now "praying" for those resting in the Spirit. Over one man in particular, he was violently pounding judo chops into his chest, and yelling, "Release, release, release!"

The commotion was such that Paul was flustered; several of the 3,000 people were on their feet, trying to see what was going on. I was seated only a few seats from the action, and thought repeatedly, *Why doesn't John have some of the ministry team take this guy to the back, and let them pray for him there?* A few days later, I asked John that very question. His answer left me speechless. He said, "I know that man; I know his heart. I know how much he loves God, and how he has committed his life to follow and serve the Lord. I have no question as to his character. Once I know that, I don't care if it's Paul Cain, or three thousand people from all over the world that get offended. If the Spirit of God chooses to move on him there and then, I'm not going to offend the Holy Spirit. All I'm going to say is, 'More Lord.'"

The Question

Where is all of this going? Again, ultimately God pours out His Spirit for end-time harvest. That doesn't mean that twos and threes will be added to our churches on a given Sunday. It doesn't mean that 20 or 30 new believers will be added in a single week. Like the early Church, we may well see 3,000 come to the Lord in a given day.

We quickly recognize that most local churches would be completely overwhelmed were that to happen. If, in a given week, the Lord added 20 newly converted pagans to our fellowships, many of us would be swamped, especially if each of those 20 reached one other unsaved friend the following week. We would then have 40 newly saved, but as yet undiscipled believers who radically change our status quo. They would be sitting in our seats, parking in our spots; it may well be that their kid will pop our kid on the nose in Sunday school.

These new converts, however, are on fire for the Lord. The first 20 each reached two unsaved friends the next week, and the second 20 each shared faith with one other friend; the attendance the third week then swells to a total of 100 new believers. The fourth week, in the favor of end-time harvest, doors and windows of faith might well be swung wide open, and those first 20 might each lead three others to Christ. The second 20 could lead two each; the third 60, just getting started, would each lead one. That would mean that the net conversion growth for the four weeks amounted to 260 new believers. These new believers would outnumber the vast majority of existing church fellowships, all in the space of a month. If this growth track slowed, and merely doubled over the course of the next month, the church would have swelled to over 4,000.

However, this kind of growth will only be assimilated by a church that is completely dependent, completely yielded, completely attentive, and completely abandoned to and unashamed of whatever the Spirit calls forth, wherever, and whenever the Lord calls. That is why John Arnott's anniversary response so humbled me. I had never seen someone live out that kind of abandon before.

A Wing and a Prayer

One night, one of the Toronto Airport Christian Fellowship's ministry team, Lynne Patch, discovered how dynamic this radical obedience can be. After her small group fellowship meeting, Lynne felt hungry. It was about midnight, and though she does not usually eat late, she drove around till she found a pizza restaurant. All she wanted was a few chicken wings; the smallest order she was allowed to place included potato wedges, which she didn't want. While she waited for her order, she turned her back on the three East Indian men working behind the counter. She found herself praying, "Lord, what am I doing here? I'm not even hungry anymore." In the reflection of the store window, she saw herself, and the three men, standing behind her. Suddenly she knew why she was there. She turned around and asked, "Do you guys know Jesus Christ?"

She did not expect their response. One of the men was pushed to the front. "He left India to come looking for Jesus! Your Jesus sent you here—tell him about your Jesus!"

Lynne began telling all three of them about the Lord, the only God. She shared the gospel with them, and when she finished, Rajah, the man pushed forward, said that he believed that Jesus is God. He believed that because Jesus had come to him in a repeated dream. He knew it was Jesus because he had seen "pictures" of the Lord.

Rajah was so moved by these recurring dreams that he had tried to attend a Christian church in India. His father, however, forbade him to do so. Rajah was a successful lawyer in his 30's, but still lived at home. Because he was under his father's authority, he was told in no uncertain terms that he would no longer be his son if he ever believed in Jesus.

Rajah not only left home, he left India, in order to find Jesus. He chose as his destination the city of Toronto, though he knew no one there. A Punjabi taxi driver took him to a local Sikh temple where he met a man who gave him a job in the pizza restaurant.

This desperate man went to several Christian churches in his area, but no one ever spoke to him. The preachers gave no altar calls, and he did not feel secure enough to ask anyone about Jesus. He had been in Canada nearly a year when Lynne met him that night.

She led him through the sinner's prayer, and assured him of God's love. Rajah came to several meetings at the Toronto Airport Christian Fellowship with her and began to be discipled. Shortly thereafter, he had to move into the heart of the city. There he began attending a local church.

* * *

If we are to respond to the works of amazing grace that the Lord purposes and orchestrates, a radical humility is called forth. As living sacrifices, our personal respectability, reputation, and control will most certainly have to be laid down. Together with the apostle Paul, we may find ourselves as "fools for Christ," assured only in the knowledge that the "folly of God is wiser than human wisdom."[12]

This is one of the reasons why there really is only one of two responses to this outpouring of God's Spirit: either one finds release or offense. After a brief time for investigation and discernment, one must conclude it is either the "Toronto Blessing" or the "Toronto Blasphemy." There really is no middle ground. Those who speak of the "Toronto Experience" are noncommittally "Laodicean."[13] To conclude "it's God, but we don't want it" is anathema.

---

12. Paul speaks at length along these lines in First Corinthians 1:18–4:21. He is speaking of the message of the cross, and his apostolic calling to preach Jesus, before whom there can be no human pride (1 Cor. 1:29).
13. See Revelation 3:14-22.

The Way Ahead

Those "in," however, find themselves continuously stretched. Some of us have recognized that when we are offended, we need to get used to it. As never before, we have learned that the Lord's question in Isaiah 43 is a rhetorical one: "See, I am doing a new thing! now it springs up; do you not perceive it?"[14] The appropriate answer? "No, Lord, we do not understand. Not quite yet Lord. Please show us more."

We can glean further revelation from one of the minor prophets, Zechariah. His name means "the Lord remembers," and he wrote to encourage the captives returning from Babylon. Many of his prophecies foretold the coming of the Messiah—the King meekly riding on a donkey; the good shepherd sold for 30 pieces of silver; the pierced One beheld; the One at whose death the sheep are scattered.[15] There are also several prophecies that anticipate and describe the second coming of the Lord—the four horsemen, the measuring of the holy city, and the two olive trees and lampstands.[16]

Chapter 14 tells of the day when "the Lord will go out and fight against the nation, fighting as on a day of battle." Two verses later, the Lord is attended by all the holy ones, and in verse 9, His majesty and dominion are declared: "The Lord will become King over all the earth; on that day He will be the only Lord and His name the only name."

The tenth chapter of Zechariah is a bridge between the first and second coming of the Lord. The text foretells

---

14. Isaiah 43:19a NIV.
15. Zechariah 9:9 and Matthew 21:9; Zechariah 11:12 and Matthew 26:15; Zechariah 12:10 and John 19:37; Zechariah 13:7 and Matthew 26:31.
16. Zechariah 1:7f. and Revelation 6:1f.; Zechariah 1:16 and Revelation 11:1-2; Zechariah 4:11-14 and Revelation 11:4-10.

God's victorious triumph over His foes; 26 times, there is the future description of what the Lord "will" do, what His people "will" be like, what destiny "will" come to pass. In this season of blessing, as we attend to where all of this is going, these verses are particularly suggestive.

In Zechariah 10, verse one, God's people are told to "ask the Lord for rain at the time of the spring rain, the Lord who makes the storm clouds...." At the outset, it is imperative that we recognize, yet again, that it is the Lord, and the Lord alone, who is the One taking the initiative. We cannot make it rain. We cannot fabricate the storm clouds. Once it is raining, however, we are invited to ask for *more*. Grace is again on the forefront. We ask for more, and the Lord promises that He will give the heavy rains, unto abundant harvest.

Radical Transformation

The third verse of this chapter begins with the declaration of God's anger over the faithlessness of His shepherds and leaders. What follows is the promise that He Himself will extend care to His flock. In the latter part of the verse, there is a most unusual metaphor—the Lord's flock will be "transformed into war horses." Regrettably, the NIV translation diminishes this dynamic: "...[the Lord will] make them a proud horse in battle." One can only wonder what has to take place to turn a cuddly little sheep into a war horse! Tongue in cheek, there will most likely be those who complain that it does not happen "decently and in order."

However one envisions becoming a war horse, Zechariah keeps his readers reeling. Four verses later, he uses another striking metaphor: God raises up an outrageous army, "with hearts gladdened *as if* with wine." Across the page, in Zechariah 9:15, this same army is described as being "roaring drunk *as if* with wine."

Before my conversion, I had a practiced knowledge of what it was to be roaring drunk with wine. That part of the picture is not a puzzle. The "as if" bit is. Why would the Lord want His army to be roaring drunk, as if with wine? Without praising alcoholic drunkenness in any way, there are a few observations that may shed some light on this peculiar text. When one is drunk, there is not much by way of striving. One's task drivenness is suppressed. "Time to go? What's your rush? Have another drink...." Further, one's inhibitions are characteristically loosened. There comes a false sense of freedom, even license; boundaries and limits fall. That is one of the reasons driving while drunk is so dangerous. A final observation: Some find that while drunk, they are not nearly so intimidated. That's why beer brawls are so common.

In the Spirit, God purposes to raise up His army. These are a people who are militant, but not full of themselves. There is no striving, and neither intimidation nor inhibition. The Lord's army is not bound by limitations, for the Lord Himself is with them. It is in this context that we understand an earlier verse, Zechariah 4:6: "...Neither by force nor by strength, but by My Spirit! says the Lord of Hosts." The Lord's army is overcome, not with wine, but with the Spirit of Jesus.

Again and again, it is declared that the Lord is the One leading. In Zechariah 10, verse 8 He says, "I shall whistle to call them in, for I have delivered them...." A complementary verse may be found in Isaiah 5:26: "He will hoist a standard as a signal to a nation far away, He will whistle them up from the ends of the earth, and they will come with all speed."

In this season of blessing, it is as if there is a catalytic acceleration to the work of God's grace right around the world. In terms of conversions, it is indeed as if the Lord has whistled, and with that clear call, the lost have found their way home. Gary Patton, of the Toronto Airport's New Life team, tells of one remarkable story.

A middle-aged Japanese businessman was facing bankruptcy in Japan. He was at his wits' end. Unexplainably, he sensed that he was to come to Canada. He contacted his travel agent, but never having been to Canada, he couldn't name a particular city as his destination. "Vancouver...? Toronto...? Montreal...?" asked his travel agent. Toronto sounded good to him.

He had no idea what he was doing, or why he was doing it. This gentleman was neither a Christian, nor a practicing religious. He had never heard of the "Toronto Blessing." Once he had disembarked, he picked up his luggage and cleared customs. Standing in the meeting area, he wondered an equivalent, "Now what?" He spoke no English.

A Japanese woman and her son were waiting for one of their family who had arrived on the same plane as the businessman. The woman felt that the Lord was telling her to go talk to this Japanese businessman, and she obeyed. As she heard his story, she had no doubt about this appointment. Once they had met their family member, she took the businessman to their home. The next day, she brought him to her church's Sunday service. Her church is the Toronto Airport Christian Fellowship.

The woman's son translated for the businessman, and when the salvation call was given, the man wanted to respond. The boy came forward with him in order to continue translating. The man accepted Jesus as his Savior and Lord, and during his altar counseling, he received the baptism of the Spirit. (It was at this point that Gary was called in to answer a few questions.)

After hearing out the story, Gary asked the boy, "Why did you bring this man here?" The answer was simple enough: " 'Cause he needed Jesus." After they prayed for the businessman some more, he walked away with a huge smile on his face, knowing EXACTLY why he was to come to Toronto. He returned to Japan the following day.

The Lord's War Horses

Many, if not most, Christians feel a sense of panic when they hear the word *evangelism*. At one end of the spectrum, there are some who are chagrined at the thought of forcing one's religious opinions on another: *A spirit of tolerance and co-existence is what is needed at the close of the millennium.* At the other end are those who feel a gnawing guilt because they have never led a single person to the Lord.

So much changes as God freely and abundantly fills us with His Spirit. In this present season of blessing, new measures of faith and faithfulness have been awakened, such that many are enabled to share the love of God with a new freedom, boldness, and authority. There has come the recognition that evangelism is not so much a task that we try to bring to conclusion, but rather, it is the work of *Christ*, in us and through us. Evangelism is by nature, supernatural!

Michael Green reflected on one of the reasons many of us have never spoken about our faith to others: we have felt too empty for the "overflow" that constitutes true evangelism. "Like tourists going through customs, we've had nothing to declare."[17] But as we have received blessing, we know as never before that God's amazing grace precedes us, undergirds us, and swirls behind us. In that knowledge, inhibitions are stripped away, such that nothing is held back. Timidity gives way to an abandoned response to the work of Christ in us, such that we seek to bring the lost into His allegiance, "...by word and deed, by the power of signs and [wonders], and by the power of the Holy Spirit...."[18] I thought

---

17. Michael Green, *Evangelism Through the Local Church* (Nashville, Tennessee: Nelson Publishers, 1992), 14.
18. Romans 15:18-19.

of the apostle's words when I heard the following testimony at a recent conference.

Leigh-Anne, September 1996

Leigh-Anne is 19 years old. She has been a Christian for almost two and a half years and presently works with the physically challenged as a care aid. Because of her background, her identity has been guarded.

* * *

"Growing up, I was never close to my family. They were alcoholics, and there was a lot of abuse in our house. My biological parents were divorced when I was two, and my mother was soon living with the man who is currently my stepfather. He is also an alcoholic. I was a very unhappy little girl, and I remember long periods of time when I refused to speak to anyone.

"I began smoking and using drugs at a very young age. I wasn't trying to be rebellious; I just couldn't find any other way to live with the hurt and the anger I felt. When I was 15 I left home to live life in "the big city," thinking I could make it on a grade nine education. It wasn't long before I ended up on the streets, confused, lost, and badly addicted to drugs. It was then that I was placed in a number of foster homes, but they never worked out. I had no idea what love was, and the only thing I seemed capable of doing was hating.

"When I turned 16, I was sent back to my hometown to live with my mother. It was only a few months later that she packed her bags and moved three provinces away. Before she left she signed documents that relinquished her guardianship. She told me I was no longer her daughter.

"Over the next year and a half, I was in more foster homes. I got involved with the occult and some really dangerous people. Before long my life was being threatened. I tried the best I could to protect myself, but to no avail. No one could help me. I remember lying in my bed one night, saying out loud, 'Okay, if You're there, God, I need You to help me because no one else can.' I scolded myself for being so stupid as to think that God was real, and never told anyone of my first 'prayer.'

"Almost a year later, I was back in the city, living on my own. My drug habit was still raging, and I became even more heavily involved in the occult. I was sitting in a coffee shop late one night with a friend, and a stranger about our age approached us. He had long hair, earrings, and a dark trench coat. He seemed pretty cool. After the introductions, Dave began to tell us about Jesus. I gave him all the attitude I could muster. He responded, 'God's telling me things about you and I bet I could give you a detailed account of your life.' I dared him to try. He told me about things there was no way he could have known. I was amazed! Dave then said, 'I also know the first time you cried out to God.' At this point I was scared because I knew that if this young guy knew about that time almost a year ago, then God was real. I tried to bluff.

" 'That's a lie. I've never cried out to God!' He closed his eyes for a minute and said, 'It was nine months and 13 days ago.' He was right. I remembered that day so clearly because I had been so scared. I went home and checked my journal—Dave was dead right—nine months, 13 days ago. I remembered that he had told me to ask God to reveal Himself to me in a dream that night. I did as he had told me to do, and God sure made Himself known! I dreamt of a golden cross appearing in the clouds before me. I knew Jesus was real!

"I then began to go to the same church that I presently attend. Because of my past, and the way I looked, I figured they'd kick me out. Instead, a complete stranger walked up to me, hugged me, and said, 'Welcome home.'

"Since that time, God has delivered me from drugs and alcohol and restored every physical side effect I got from drugs. He has taught me how to speak blessing instead of curses, and each day He softens my heart more and teaches me more about His perfect love. Maybe I didn't believe in God, but He believed in me. He's saved me from so much, time and time again, and I'm so thankful. He even helped me go back and finish high school! His mercies are new each day!

"As I've walked with the Lord, He's filled a place of emptiness with an immense love for His people. Whether we know Him or not, we are all His children, and He desperately wants us to know Him. The more I love Jesus, the more I love His people and, in turn, the more desperately I want His children to know Him.

"My friend Donna and I often go out for coffee after work. On the way to the coffee shop, we pray for a 'divine appointment,' a meeting with a stranger who doesn't know Jesus. We ask the Lord to interrupt our evening with whatever we can do for Him. We sit down and talk, go about our normal business, and wait for Jesus to arrange a meeting.

"One night in particular, we were in the restaurant, and Jesus really drew our attention to our waitress. We began to pray for her, and Jesus showed me in a picture that she was bulimic. I struggled with talking to her about it but Donna encouraged me a lot. When our waitress came back, I made a beginning. 'We were just praying for you and I believe the Lord just showed me that you're bulimic. Could we pray for you?' She became very defensive and rude, and denied that she had ever even considered doing anything so horrible to change her appearance. I was devastated. I thought I had made God look ridiculous. Ten minutes later, she came back to our table. She was crying, and explained how she had just been discharged from the hospital for bulimia. She was suicidal and had exhausted all avenues of help. She let us pray for her and Jesus came and touched her. PRAISE GOD!

"About a year ago, our church did a conference in Golden, British Columbia. During the weekend, we did an outreach in the park. We gave out hamburgers and drinks, and met a lot of young people that afternoon. We invited them all to the evening meeting. They pointed to a young guy in black across the park and said, 'Don't invite Shawn. He's a satanist.' My first reaction? God LOVES satanists! I went over to invite him, and he said that Tom, a guy from our band, had already invited him, and we could just leave him alone.

"That night, I arrived late for the meeting. Worship had already started. As I walked up the church steps, Shawn came running out in a panic. 'Something's happening in there! I can feel it! As soon as I went in I started shaking. What's going on?!' My friend Jen stayed with him while I went to get Tom to come and pray. After prayer and conversation, Shawn had become the newest member of our family in Christ! God had sovereignly drawn Shawn to Himself because He knew Shawn's heart. Jesus knows us better than we know ourselves and He will do whatever it takes to reach us.

"In August of this year, our church held a renewal meeting in one of our local parks. They had asked a few people to share their testimonies and before long, it was my turn. As I spoke, Jesus filled me with so much love for people that I began to cry. He laid it on my heart to invite people up for prayer. Guess who responded? Not the most intelligent people, not the most gifted people, not the most spiritual people, but little children. They came running up to me, pulling at me, saying, 'We want to get prayed for!' What a picture of the Lord's heart.

"Recently, I was hanging out on Granville Street (skid row) in Vancouver, with a mercy ministry from another church. A young guy, John, came up to me and was basically laughing at me because I was a Christian. He seemed to be the mouthy tough guy of his group of friends. I said, 'Hey man. Can I pray for you?' He let me, thinking I was giving him more ammunition for his mockery. I began to pray that God would shine His light. Then I told him, 'Ask Jesus if He loves you.' He hesitated. 'Go ahead, ask Him.' He did, and Jesus responded. I can't say I know exactly how (that's between John and the Lord) but his face softened and tears began to stream down his face. John is now walking with the Lord and attending a local church.

"I realize that my generation is not all that pleasant to look at, and we're not exactly kind or eloquent. But we have nothing left to hope in, nothing to believe in, and nothing to look forward to. Sexual and physical abuse, drug addiction, and abortion are normal in our lives, and we don't know how to live through it. So, we internalize it and become angry and bitter towards adults, government, and any type of authority figure. It's only because we are hurt and dying and overcome with hopelessness. So, who's going to love us? Who's going to believe in us and love us back to life?

"I believe that God has big plans for my generation and that He's gifted us and called us to it. But the workers are few and not all of us have found the way to freedom yet. Do you realize that the reason why we have systems like foster homes and welfare is because the church hasn't done its job? GOD BELIEVES IN US! Please, I implore you, let Him show you that.

"I also know that God believes in His Church, and so do I. During this renewal movement, I have been blessed to see God work miracles in the Body. He is reconstructing cold and resentful hearts so that they can love again. He is pulling down walls of division and stereotypes, and dealing with hidden sin. He's giving His Bride joy again, and consuming her with passion for her Groom, Jesus. I believe we are all called to witness to this world, but how can we if we don't have love? God's Spirit is moving and equipping His Church with more than enough love for this world, if only we are willing.

"God loves all His people more than we could ever comprehend. If you ask God to use you, He will, because He knows what state this world is in. The days are short and the Lord desperately wants to restore His Church that it might be effective in reaching an otherwise hopeless generation."

* * *

In Joel 2:28 and Acts 2:17, the Father's sovereign purpose is declared: "In the last days, says God, I will pour out My Spirit on all mankind; and your sons and daughters shall prophesy; your young men shall see visions, and your old men shall dream dreams." The outpouring of His Spirit is to one end only—that "...everyone who calls on the name of the Lord will be saved."[19]

Leigh-Anne's life and witness are a grace-filled demonstration of Joel 2 and Acts 2. Through Spirit-initiated words, pictures, visions, and dreams, these prophetic stirrings and urgings move us to reach out with supernatural authority and freedom. In the power of the Spirit, we love, speak, and bless, confident that the Lord goes before us, opening doors, and initiating *kairos* moments, such that the lost find themselves found in the love of the Father.

Grace-based evangelism is not so much a particular methodology to be learned or a strategic program to be followed. But as has been demonstrated through all the testimonies, neither is it a totally passive "waiting on God" that

19. Acts 2:21 NIV.

keeps the gospel unspoken. Again and again, the Spirit releases the authority and the grace for the Lord's witnesses to ask the noontime questions: Do you know Jesus? Would you like to?"

Part of me, however, remains frustrated, for there is a sense that I still do not know "how" to win the lost. It is not for lack of content. The following appendix may serve those who do not know what to say when someone is ready to receive Christ.

Although we must be able to tell someone the basics of the gospel of Jesus Christ, it is not we who do the soul-winning. Rather, ours is the humble and surrendered recognition that salvation comes only as Jesus said it would: "No one can come to Me unless he is drawn by the Father."[20] In this, we are totally *dependent*, not totally passive. The Lord has called us as His witnesses, and in this season of blessing, we have so much *more* to declare. As we open our hearts to receive an ever greater revelation of our Father's love for us, we receive a graced impregnation that, when nurtured, yields fruitfulness.

All around us are divinely ordained moments of grace...and as we have compassion on the next one, and attend to what the Lord purposes in this particular moment, we will discover greater faith, and freedom, and ever more grace.

Soli Deo Gloria[21]

---

20. John 6:44.
21. To God alone be the glory.

Appendix

Faith Sharing

* * *

If we have compassion on the next one, and if we are attending to what the Spirit is calling forth in our midst, sooner or later, someone will say to us: "I've been watching you. There's something to this Christianity business. I want what you have. How do I become a Christian?" Alternatively, the Spirit will convince us that it is time to ask, "Do you know Jesus?"

The following may serve those who do not know what to say next.

In John's Gospel, chapter 1, verse 10, we read, "He [Jesus] was in the world; but the world, though it owed its being to Him, did not recognize Him."

1. "Recognize"

When we strip Christian faith right down, the first thing we have to say is that being a Christian means recognizing Jesus. John puts it in the negative here—the world, the unbelieving world, did NOT recognize Jesus. When we turn that around, a believer, a follower of Jesus, DOES recognize Him.

What does it mean to recognize someone? It means to know something about that person. You can't "recognize" a stranger.

In terms of recognizing Jesus, what do we have to know about Him? Remember, we are keeping this simple. What needs to be recognized in Jesus? Let me suggest this: Jesus is the Son of God, and the Giver of Life. We need to recognize that Jesus wants to change our lives. Jesus shows us what life is really meant to be like—what love, peace, joy, and freedom truly are. Stripped right down, we need to recognize that in Jesus, there is a quality to life, a desirability to life, that is missing without Him.

However, we can't stop there. It is quite possible to recognize that someone loves us, but be totally unmoved by that love. John 1:11 makes this very declaration: "He [Jesus] [entered His own realm], and His own people would not [receive] Him."

2. "Receive"

Not only do we have to recognize Jesus, we have to receive His love. We ask Jesus, the Life-changer, to change OUR lives. What Jesus most changes in our lives is our sin, all that has mashed and marred our living. He takes all of that on Himself, dying in our place, so that we can know His sinless life, as He lives in us. He is willing to exchange His life for ours, because He loves each of us so much.

It doesn't stop there. In John 1:12 we read: "But to all who did [receive] Him, to those who [believed in His name], He gave the right to become children of God."

3. "Believe in His Name"

To recognize and receive Jesus is not enough. There is a personal response called forth. Recognition and reception of Jesus reorients our lives such that we live under a new "name," a new authority. Most of us have trouble with authority; we don't like being told what to do, even if our best interests are on the line. That's one of the reasons many people never "believe in the name of Jesus."

What does "believing in His name" mean for our daily lives? It means that we decide to name Christ as THE authority in our lives. Maybe we hold our hands open, as a symbol of our abandonment to Him; maybe we simply say "Yes, Lord." Then, as the Spirit of Jesus lives in us, He shows us what that "Yes, Lord" involves

1. Recognizing Jesus, and wanting the life He has to give.

2. Receiving Jesus, and accepting the love He brings to our lives.

3. Believing in the name of Jesus, and allowing His Spirit to transform our lives, saying our "Yes" to what He wills for us.

Bob George puts it all in one sentence: "Jesus Christ laid down His life *for us*, so that He could give His life *to us*, so that He could live His life *through us*."[1]

---

1. Bob George, *Basic Christianity* (Eugene, Oregon: Harvest House Publishers, 1989), 174.

Select Bibliography

Augustine. *Confessions.* Trans. J.G. Pilkerton. Nicene and Post-Nicene Fathers, First Series, vol. 1. Peabody, Massachusetts: Hendrickson Publishers, 1994.

Evans, Eifion. *The Welsh Revival of 1904.* Worcester: Evangelical Press of Wales, 1969.

Green, Michael. *Evangelism Through the Local Church.* Nashville, Tennessee: Thomas Nelson, Pub., 1992.

Jones, Brynmor Pierce. *An Instrument of Revival: The Complete Life of Evan Roberts 1878-1951.* South Plainfield, New Jersey: Bridge Publishing, 1995.

_____. *Voices From the Welsh Revival 1904-1905.* Bridgend: Evangelical Press of Wales, 1995.

Jones, Marty Lloyd. *Revival.* Wheaton, Illinois: Crossway Books, 1987.

McGavran, Donald. *Understanding Church Growth*, 3rd. ed. Grand Rapids, Michigan: William B. Eerdmans Pub. Co., 1990.

The Revival of Religion: Addresses by Scottish Evangelical Leaders. Edinburgh: The Banner of Truth Trust, 1840/1984.

Synan, Vincent, ed. *Aspects of Pentecostal-Charismatic Origins.* Plainfield, New Jersey: Logos International, 1975.